The Successful A

Gordon Wells had his first book published in 1963. Since then he has – in his 'spare' time – produced more than twenty non-fiction books including the best-selling *Magazine Writer's Handbook* and the management text *How to Communicate*. He is now working full-time at writing and associated activities.

Some other books by Gordon Wells

The Craft of Writing Articles
Writers' Questions Answered
The Magazine Writer's Handbook
The Book Writer's Handbook

How to Communicate

Traffic Engineering
Highway Planning Techniques
Comprehensive Transport Planning

The Successful Author's Handbook

Gordon Wells

PAPERMAC

First published 1981 by
THE MACMILLAN PRESS LTD
London and Basingstoke

First published in 1981 by
PAPERMAC,
a division of Macmillan Publishers Limited
Associated companies in Auckland, Delhi, Dublin, Gaborone, Hamburg, Harare, Hong Kong, Johannesburg, Kuala Lumpur, Lagos, Manzini, Melbourne, Mexico City, Nairobi, New York, Singapore and Tokyo

Reprinted 1982, 1983, 1984, 1986

New edition 1989
Reprinted 1990, 1991

Typeset in 11/12pt Baskerville by
STYLESET LIMITED
Salisbury, Wiltshire

ISBN 0–333–49947–6

A CIP catalogue record for this book is available from the British Library.

Printed and bound in Hong Kong

Contents

1 The basic idea

Many specialists and academics dream of writing a book about their subject. So too do hobbyists and amateur historians. This is fine. Around twenty-five thousand new non-fiction books are published each year in Britain alone, yet there seems always to be room for one more good one.

And, while the five thousand new fiction books published each year attract the most literary and critical attention, the non-fiction books are often better sellers. The average first novel will only sell a couple of thousand copies; very few first novels are taken up by book clubs, paperback publishers and film producers. There are few writers like Hammond Innes, Harold Robbins or Len Deighton. Many more write one novel and then fade away – broke. The greatest best-seller of all time is the Bible – and that is non-fiction. P. A. Samuelson's *Economics* (McGraw-Hill) has sold several million copies, all over the world, in ten editions plus translations. Ronald Ridout has written over three hundred school texts, and has thereby made himself a small fortune.

At the more mundane level of us ordinary mortals, almost all general educational (that is, below university level) texts should sell around ten thousand copies over five years. Other non-fiction books–for example on management, a specialist subject or a hobby – ought to sell the whole of a three to five thousand first print run.

So, writing a specialist non-fiction book is a worthwhile occupation. Many people dream about it; few actually get down to it; fewer still complete the task. It entails a lot of hard work. There is a right way and a wrong way to go about it. This book will help you to do it the right way. It cannot help you to write a fiction book. Nor can it guarantee that you will find a publisher for the non-fiction book you have in mind – there may be no market for it. But at least you will understand why no publisher would take it.

To write a complete book, without thought of the market, and then start hawking it around the publishers is amateurish. That book may never get published. This book is about the professional approach to non-fiction writing, as summarised in figure 1.1. The professional approach will mean, among other things, seldom if ever, being left with an 'unsold' book.

To be specific, this book is aimed at the specialist who wants to write a book about some aspect of his work; at the teacher or lecturer who sees a need for a new approach to his subject; at the manager who hopes to write about management techniques and at the man with a lot of knowledge to pass on about a fairly technical hobby. Great literary ability is not necessary; accuracy of information and clarity of expression are more important. The principles – but perhaps not quite all the techniques – will apply equally to any other non-fiction book. They will not apply to the writing, production and selling of a novel.

Why write a book?

To survive the hard labour and the trauma of getting your book into the bookshops, you need a good reason for writing it. So why do you want to write a book? Money? You would probably do better moonlighting as a window-cleaner. Status, kudos, recognition? Certainly these can be an important part of your reason for writing, just as money too will be an important part of the reason. But neither money nor kudos

1 Develop an idea for a book and consider whether there is a potential market for it.

2 Research the subject thoroughly.

3 Prepare a detailed synopsis for the book and a 'statement of objectives' – who the book is intended for, and why it is needed.

4 Reach agreement with a publisher on the synopsis – amending it as necessary in the light of the publisher's commercial judgement.

5 Write a sample chapter or two for the publisher's approval.

6 On receipt of a contract from the publisher, and not before, start writing the balance of the book, in line with the agreed synopsis.

7 Deliver an accurate, neat, typed, manuscript, plus all necessary supplementary material, to the publisher, by or before his deadline date.

8 Work with the publisher on any necessary revisions, editing, etc., through the proofs, to

9 Publication.

10 Keep your eyes open for possible sales ideas and leads.

Fig 1.1 The professional approach to non-fiction writing – in a nutshell.

should be the main reason for writing a book. Neither is enough to see you through, and both are likely to generate 'hack' writing. Brutally, the main reason for writing a book almost has to be a certain amount of egotism. You have to have a conviction that you can produce something (a book) that others will find useful and of value. You should also get some pleasure in stringing words together. You want to write your book because 'you can't not': there is a need for it.

Conviction and delight are not enough on their own. You must add to them the prospect of both money and kudos. Let me make quite clear my concept of an essential conviction though. No writer should ever harbour a conceited or over-inflated opinion of his ability. A modest attitude of searching for truth is more appropriate, if hard to maintain. At the same time, no writer will fail to look with justifiable pride at 'his book' – a book with his name on the cover. But a major criterion of writing success should always be a book's sales – which eventually mean money for the writer. If a book is not written to sell, it will not be published. That means not only no money, but no 'name on the cover' either.

Let us continue to think about money. It has been said many times before, but it needs to be repeated again and again: never, *never*, NEVER pay for your book to be published. If a book is worth publishing – and we come to this in more detail later – you will eventually find a publisher. There are something like five hundred separate publishers in Britain alone – without new books to publish they will eventually go out of business. They depend on a continuing supply of acceptable book manuscripts. 'Publishers' who produce books against payment by their authors – 'vanity publishers' – are usually little more than enterprising printers. They seldom, if ever, go out of their way to sell their books; most bookshops recognise their names and don't bother to stock their otherwise unpublishable offerings.

There are many stories about people who have written, for instance, their memoirs, withdrawn all their savings and paid a printer to produce their work as a book – and then start searching for a 'publisher'. There are stories of people with studies crammed full of unsold – and unsellable – books that they have paid to have printed. But the standard advice to find a publisher who will publish at his own expense, and pay the writer, has been given so often that by now the author who has had his book printed at his own expense can almost always be written off as a crank.

A real publisher stakes both his money and his reputation on each book that he considers worthy of publication under his imprint.

The other side of the 'don't pay' coin is equally important. Samuel Johnson is reported – in Boswell's *Life of Johnson* – to have said it first: 'No man but a blockhead ever wrote, except for money.' That is – never write for publication without payment. This side of the coin needs a minor qualification, however. It is occasionally worth writing, for instance a technical paper, for publication without payment in a learned journal, if publication generates kudos in your job or profession.

So, we are writing 'because we must', but expecting reasonable payment for our efforts. That *ethos* puts us squarely in the market place. It requires us to behave like professionals: to present, display and sell our wares efficiently; to think commercially; and to meet the reasonable requirements of the 'purchaser'. And in the initial stages, the purchaser is the publisher.

The publisher is willing to publish your book because he believes that it will sell to the public or to schools and colleges. He relies on these sales to make his profit; without profit he will go out of business. He considers that the subject will interest large numbers of people – sufficiently for them to buy a book about it.

It is a very useful – and often salutary – exercise to think to yourself whether you would buy a book such as the one you propose, if you saw it advertised, or in a bookshop, written by someone else. Or, if you are a lecturer or teacher, would you recommend it to your students? This is what guides the publisher. And he invests a lot of money in your book.

A book about what?

If you are convinced that you want to write a book, you

probably know just what you want to write about. But think about this a little more. You must know your subject really well if you are to write a book about it. There is no better way of ensuring that you know a subject really well than by having to write about it. All those minor points that you glossed over in your mind must now be explained in detail. That is when you discover, to your horror, that you didn't really understand it after all. In compensation though, once you have 'mugged up' those bits you didn't understand, in order to write about them, you will be that much more knowledgeable yourself.

Define the subject of your book as clearly as possible. Write it down on a sheet of paper. Break it down into sub-themes. Do you know enough about each of these sub-themes to explain them in detail? Have you in fact broken the subject down merely into the aspects of which you are yourself aware, or are they really all the aspects? In other words, are you thinking of the whole of the subject, or just that part that interests you?

It is not necessarily wrong to restrict the subject to the part that interests you. The necessary qualification is that it must be a part that stands alone in its own right. To explain that with an example: it could be quite acceptable to think of a book about practical gardening that excluded all reference to the science of soil chemistry. It would almost certainly not be acceptable to write about practical gardening without discussion, for instance, about timetables for planting or about fertiliser requirements.

Another matter that needs to be thought about at this stage is whether or not the subject as you define it is worth a book to itself. Without being much of a gardener, I think that it would be hard to write a whole book about weeding, or about garden-fertilisers. (But that statement is almost an invitation to some enthusiastic writer-gardener to prove me wrong.) Both of these gardening functions would presumably be essential ingredients, however, in a general gardening book.

It is not sufficient merely to think about whether a subject is big enough to write about though. Is it a big enough subject for people to buy a book about it? How many people? You may be the world's leading expert on double-ended oojima-flips – but is anyone else in the whole world interested in them? Even the most specialist of publishers will hope to sell a couple of thousand copies of any book he publishes, and many of these sales would be to libraries, implying multiple readership. You need to think of a subject that will appeal to at least several thousand people.

If your basic idea is too small or too narrow to warrant a whole book in its own right, and you are not yourself capable of widening the scope, consider collaboration. It is sometimes possible to write a book jointly with another equally narrow specialist, producing a very worthwhile, saleable, joint effort. (It is wise though, to agree very clearly between yourselves, in advance, your individual responsibilities and the apportionment of the royalties. For more on royalties, see chapter 10.)

Another possible way of obtaining improved coverage of a subject is to negotiate with a colleague to write a specific chapter for you, on an aspect that you cannot deal with yourself. (You should retain the right to edit his text to ensure that is conforms to the style of the rest of the book, which is yours. It is often possible to compensate a one-chapter collaborator with a lump sum payment rather than with a share of future royalties.) There is also the possibility of a handbook – a compilation of chapters, each written by a specialist in that field, the whole book being organised and pulled together by an editor. This concept is further examined in chapters 4 and 6.

Another important factor in considering the basic coverage of the book is the educational level at which it is pitched. This is part of the process of identifying the potential reader, which is explained further in chapter 3. If you are writing a book about computers, the level of coverage would be very different if the potential reader were a scientist or a schoolchild. (My own knowledge of computer technology was totally inadequate for me to write about computers for scientists, but I was able to write a simple – and successful – children's book explaining what a computer is and what it does.)

Competition

At this preliminary stage of the 'getting into print' process, when all you have is a germ of an idea for a book, it is essential to investigate the opposition – the competition. Almost inevitably there is already a book on the same subject; there may be several. You need to be aware of all of them before you start on your own book. In your own specialist field you will know the better competitive books – you may not know them all. So check.

Visit your local library; browse through the relevant sections of the shelves; chat up the librarian. Investigate the stock of your local bookshop – or nearest technical bookshop, for many bookshops do not deal with the sort of book we are considering. Perhaps make friends with the bookshop proprietor; he will be able to tell you of other books on 'your' subject – he may be able to advise you which ones sell best, and why. Go through the bibliographies at the rear of similar texts in your own possession. And at least glance at as many of the competitive books as you can lay your hands on.

You need to get a 'feel' of the opposition: at what level they are pitched, how broadly or in how much detail they cover the subject, and whether, in your view, they are good value for money. If you owned a copy of each of these competitive books, would you still be prepared to buy – or recommend to your students – the one you are now proposing to write? It is important, in the case of academic textbooks for which the size of the total market is virtually fixed, to be sure of how and why your book can carve out a new slice of that market. There is little room for the overall market to grow; when money is short the market is more likely to contract. Sales of your book will have to be at the expense of someone else's book. Whose, and why?

Your book is obviously, in your view, going to be better – in some, perhaps small, way – than the competition. (If not, why are you writing it?) You need to be able to explain just why your book is needed: which vacant niche in the wall of information it will fill. Maybe your book will explain the subject more simply; maybe it will go into more detail about one important aspect of the subject. (Perhaps it should therefore concentrate on that alone?) Maybe you can identify a class of reader not yet, or not adequately, catered for.

There will always be room for another good book on any subject, as long as it is better in some way, as long as it fills a previously unfilled need.

Do not treat lightly this survey of competitive books. It is very important for two reasons. Firstly, it will give you ideas on how to handle parts of the subject in your own book – or show you how not to handle them. And, of course, you will inevitably pick up snippets of information you did not previously know. (But see also the comments on plagiarism in chapter 2.) Secondly, later in the book-writing process, when you have attracted the interest of a publisher, he will want to know in what ways your book will be better than the competition. He will need to decide how to direct his sales campaign for your book – to convince owners of one or more of the competitive books to buy yours too. You can only answer these queries from knowledge.

Summary

(1) Writing a book is a lot of hard work. It is wise to sort out, early on, why you want to write one. The best reasons are fourfold: a wish to pass on one's knowledge, an enjoyment of stringing words together, a desire for kudos, and a liking for money. Without acknowledging all four reasons, the approach may well be amateurish.

(2) While you may not make a lot of money from a non-fiction book, the financial side of getting into print is most important. Unless a book is likely to make money, it is unlikely to get published. Writers should 'think commercial' and 'act professional'.

(3) If a publisher cannot be found to take on and finance a book, it is almost certainly not worth publishing. NEVER pay to have your own book published.

(4) Never write without the expectation of payment or, in the case of occasional learned papers, of professional kudos.

(5) A book must deal with all aspects of its subject; the subject itself must warrant a book.

(6) Study other books on the same subject – the competition; identify the respects in which your book will be better. If not better – why write it?

2

Research - collecting and organising material

As has already been made clear, this book is about writing non-fiction. The dictionary defines non-fiction as 'literary matter based directly on fact'. The most important thing about a non-fiction book is the factual information it conveys. The literary style is of less importance, as long as it is clear. The quality of the information is what matters; inaccuracy is a cardinal sin for a non-fiction writer.

The need for research

A non-fiction writer is therefore, necessarily and above all, someone who collects information about his chosen subject – or subjects. He must know all there is to know in his field – subject always to the *level* at which he works. This can mean detailed specialised knowledge of a very narrow subject – knowing more than anyone else about an esoteric subject such as 'the production of gold amalgams in zero-gravity conditions'. It can also mean knowing more than is ordinarily necessary about all aspects of a broad subject. This would cover, for instance, a teacher of mathematics who knows more than is required, about every part of a college mathematics syllabus, without having detailed or 'high level' knowledge of any single part.

The non-fiction writer needs to collect all sorts of information about his subject. He needs to be aware of most, if not all, of the books that have been published in his field. But books alone are not enough. It is important to be up-to-date, which means regularly collecting material from magazines and other journals. Clearly, the collection and retention of material is a lengthy – and continuing – process.

It is most unusual – and potentially disastrous – to decide on a specialist subject for a book and only then to start collecting material. A writer is well-advised to select his book subject from within his existing interests; he will probably still need to collect more detailed specific material, but he will not be starting from scratch. This is really only another way of repeating the well-known advice to 'write about what you know'.

That advice about working within existing areas of interest, needs some explanation and qualification. It is clearly appropriate to an idea for a book about 'gold amalgams in zero-gravity', or college mathematics. But what about a book about 'walking in Wales'? Surely all that this would entail in the way of research is to go walking with your eyes open? I suggest however that an inveterate non-walker like myself, almost totally disinterested in both flora and fauna, and in archaeology, would be at a considerable disadvantage. A keen walker, interested in the lesser spotted ragwort, the birds, the bees, and the piles of old stones, would have a good head-start on me. He would probably have sufficient background knowledge to sort out appropriate material about Wales before starting on any actual 'walking research'.

To reassure those put off by the thought of having to re-invent the wheel or re-discover penicillin before they can write a book, let me hasten to define research for writers. Research, to a writer, means the collection and collating of information. It need not entail, but of course does not preclude, physical or mental *discovery*. A writer is not necessarily required to extend the bounds of all human knowledge – merely the knowledge of this reader.

An area of research important to many writers, and particularly to those writing academic text-books, yet often overlooked, is the appropriate examination syllabus. If contemplating, for instance, a basic economics text, it is obviously necessary to ensure that the common core of all relevant examination syllabuses is adequately covered in the proposed book. If the book can cover all of several 'competing' syllabuses, this must further improve its sales potential. A check on the existence, and on the content, of any relevant syllabuses is also a good idea before writing almost any technical book. Somewhere, there may be an examination syllabus covering 'the production of amalgams'. If so, it might be worth slightly adjusting the content of the book on 'gold amalgams in zero-gravity' to cover in full that part of the syllabus dealing with that speciality.

Plagiarism and copyright

The problems of plagiarism and copyright are frequently raised in the context of writers' research – and rightly so. But they need not be too much of a constraint. It was once, flippantly, explained to me that if I only read one book before I wrote something, the result probably constituted plagiarism. If I read two books, it was legitimate research. This is over-simplistic but contains a measure of common sense.

There can be no copyright of a fact, nor of an idea as such. The copyright will apply to the form in which the fact or idea is communicated. If therefore a writer wishes to *quote* from the work of another he may infringe the copyright of the original author. If he paraphrases the work of another author to any extent, he may be liable to a charge of plagiarism. In both cases the question is one of extent.

To cite examples: an unauthorised direct quotation in

someone else's book, of the whole of the previous two paragraphs, would certainly be an infringement of copyright. A technical paper based on the unacknowledged research work of another would also undoubtedly be plagiarism – the 'author' would, if nothing else, be attracting undeserved kudos.

It is not enough merely to quote the source of the quotation from another's work. A credit line does not excuse an infringement of copyright. It is sometimes difficult to avoid unintentional quotation of a few words however. Although legal experts will caution against any direct quotation – whether credited or not – there are rules of thumb. Commonly, up to about fifty words are quoted, with credit, without copyright permission. When in doubt, any non-fiction writer should, of course, seek the permission of the copyright owner to quote extracts.

Plagiarism is less easy to define. A lengthy, close, paraphrase of another's work would be liable to a charge of plagiarism. Again, when in doubt, seek permission from the writer or copyright owner – and generally avoid lengthy or over-close paraphrases of others' work.

Research sources

As we have already said, a non-fiction writer cannot operate on book research alone. The sources of his information-collecting – both continuing and specific to a new book – will include:

- personal experience
- original research, including questionnaires, interviews and personal correspondence
- material from journals, magazines, etc. – including, as appropriate, newspapers
- books – one's own, and those in libraries.

No one source will normally be sufficient on its own. (See figure 2.1)

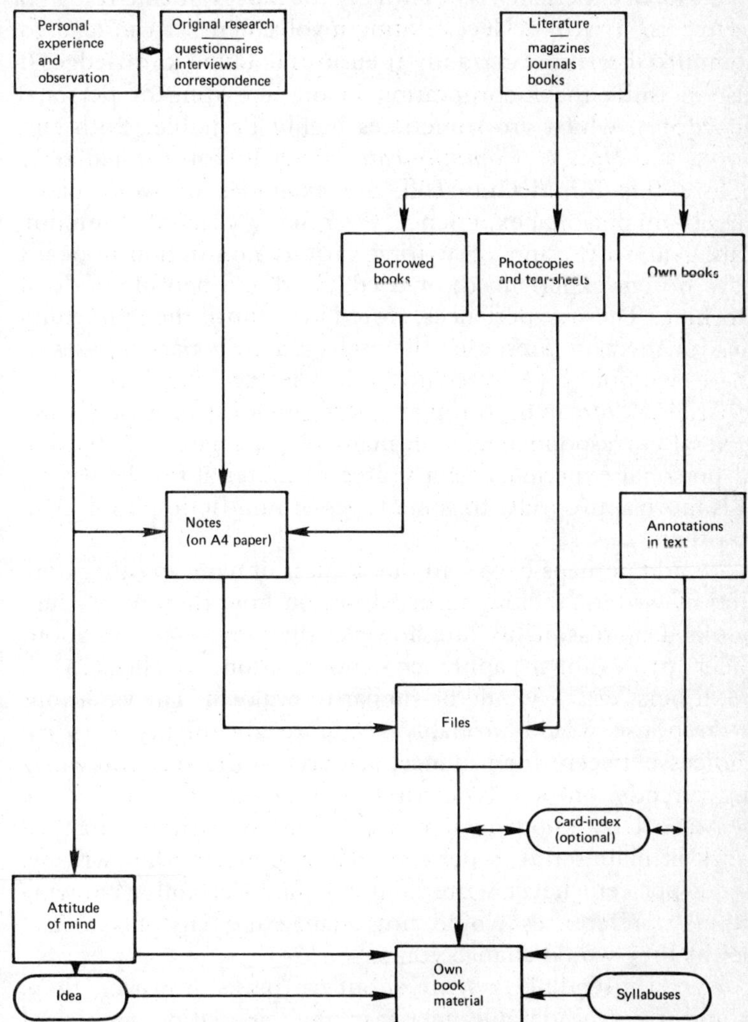

Fig 2.1 The non-fiction writer's research process, as a flow chart.

Personal experience is potentially the most valuable research source to a writer. Necessitating involvement, it can lead to committed writing; certainly it ensures detailed knowledge. It also permits the incorporation in one's writing of personal anecdotes, which are sometimes highly desirable. Both this book, and *How to Communicate* which I wrote immediately before this for McGraw-Hill, are examples of work based largely on personal experience. Over many years of communicating at work, and of writing various non-fiction books, I have noted, experienced, or tried, good and bad methods of working. These experiences, stored away until the opportunities for their use presented themselves, are the partial bases of these two books. (And see below for 'storage' details.)

Original research, through questionnaires, interviews and general correspondence is, in many ways, a natural extension of personal experience as a source of material for the writer. It is more appropriate to some types of non-fiction book than to others.

I could perhaps have sent out a questionnaire to other non-fiction writers, seeking information on how they write their books. I am reasonably sure however that any responses about their professional approach – preparation, dealings with publishers, etc. – would be similar to my own. The variations in response would probably relate to the highly personal choices between, for instance, manuscript drafting and working directly onto a typewriter. Would you, the reader, be better off by knowing that *x* per cent of writers surveyed work in manuscript, *y* per cent play pop music while writing, and *z* per cent never write before 7 pm? Certainly, knowing others' preferences would not change my customs, and I doubt they would change yours.

Were I intending to write about car parks, however, there would be considerable merit in my circulating municipal authorities with a questionnaire about park sizes, tariffs and operating costs. The tabular material derived from such a survey would be likely to interest and be of value to the reader of a technical book about parking. In similar vein, a recent book about weddings was partly based on direct interviews with two hundred married couples of all ages. Again, a worthwhile piece of original research. For an academic textbook it is wise to consult others in the same field, for advice on, for instance, the importance they attach to different aspects of the subject, and to develop a consensus view of 'best' teaching and presentational methods.

Most specialists keep themselves fairly up-to-date with goings-on in at least that part of their field that interests them. Usually this entails reading the appropriate specialist journal. Therein will be reviews of most of the new books in your field – so at least you will know what you have not yet read. It is also important not to neglect small news items relevant to your discipline – in daily papers, etc. Cut them out, mark them with the source, stick them on larger sheets of paper, and keep them.

Few specialists themselves purchase all the relevant journals; many are circulated among others in the same field within an organisation. And here we can all raise up our hearts in a paean to the great god Xerox. Were it not for photocopying we would need to write our own, and copious, notes far more frequently. So long as photocopies are made solely for personal research purposes, are not too long, nor for sale, and only a single copy is made, then they are unlikely to be considered an infringement of copyright. Photocopies are cheap to make; they should form an important part of every non-fiction writer's research 'library'. When possible, of course, tear out and retain magazine pages without copying – 'tear sheets'. We consider storage methods and 'recall' systems later in this chapter.

And finally, as research sources, books. Every writer should read, avidly, all works in his field. (And personal books should always be annotated – underlining important sections and making marginal explanatory notes.) All relevant books should be read even if the writer considers them to be at too low a level to interest him, or not quite within his speciality. He needs to read the low-level books in order to achieve an understanding of how other writers handle 'his' subject. He needs to read around and outside the fringes of his particular speciality to ensure that he can himself cover the whole of his subject in adequate depth. To clarify that advice with an example: a specialist traffic engineer should probably be reading about public transport operational management. This would ensure that he at least understood the effects of traffic management measures on bus operations.

No writer, however, will wish to buy his own copy of every book on his subject. Some he will borrow. It is neither financially practicable nor legally permissible to photocopy large chunks of a book – nor is a simple copy or extract what is usually required. Of far more use to a non-fiction writer would be a few pages of notes, summarising whole chapters, plus the odd brief verbatim extract.

Notes

Nothing, perhaps, is more valuable to a non-fiction writer than his own personal notes. Every writer will develop his own method of note-taking as he progresses, but a few hints may help the beginner. A writer's notes need to be somewhat different from those of a non-writer.

A prime essential in any writer's note is the source. It is recommended that the full title of the book and the author's name be the first things to be noted down. This is common sense and common courtesy – to be able to cite the source. But for a writer this is not enough; he needs also to record the publisher's name and the copyright date and edition. Any citation in our book must include all these details.

It will also be found particularly useful to record classification details of borrowed books. On page (iv) in the prelims (see Chapter 8), the reverse of the title page, will be found most of the necessary information. In newer books all necessary details are included as the 'British Library – or Library of Congress – Cataloguing in Publication' Data. This 'CIP' data includes the ISBN (International Standard Book Number) and the Dewey and Library of Congress classifications of the book.

The ISBN system, operated in Britain by the Standard Book Numbering Agency Ltd, uses a ten-digit number unique to each book (and edition). This number enables the book trade and the library world to identify singularly the 'language-area' of publication (not the country), the publisher, and the book itself. The paperback edition of this book for instance has the ISBN on the back cover and on page iv in the CIP data: 0 333 30463 2. This is translated:

0	333	30463	2
0 = English-speaking world	333 = Macmillan	30463 = this book	2 = a check digit for 'proving' the whole ISBN number
	14 = Penguin	(A Penguin book would have a six-digit number	
1 = spare for English	07 = McGraw-Hill	. . .	
2 = French-speaking	85264 = Charles Griffin & Co (Specialist publisher of statistics books, and my books on transportation planning.)	A Griffin book would have only a three-digit number, to retain the overall 10-digit consistency.)	
3 = German-speaking			

The Dewey and Library of Congress classifications will enable you quickly to relocate a book on the library shelves, should you wish to borrow it again. Most British libraries have adopted the Dewey Decimal system of classification. This classifies books under ten main classes, which can be subdivided again and again, to as many as six or seven digits, subdivided by decimal points. The main classes are:

000 General Works		
100 Philosophy and Psychology		
200 Religion		
300 Social Sciences		
400 Language (Philology)		
500 Pure Science		
600 Useful Arts (Technology)	610 Medicine	
700 Fine Arts	620 Engineering	621 Mechanical Eng.
800 Literature	630 Agriculture	622 Mining Eng.
900 History	etc.	623 Military Eng.
		624 Civil Engineering
		etc.

This book, on page iv, is given the Dewey classification 808, meaning:

8 Literature
80 Rhetoric (composition) and collections
808 Rhetoric technique of oral and written communication for clarity and aesthetic pleasure

The Library of Congress classification system is widely used, particularly in America. It uses a combination of capital letters and numbers to identify classifications. The use of letters rather than numbers obviously extends the range from Dewey's ten main classes to a potential twenty-six. The main Library of Congress classes are:

A Encyclopedias and reference books
B Philosophy, Psychology, Religion
C Antiquities, Biography
D History
E/F American History
G Geography and Anthropology
H Social Sciences, Economics, Sociology
I Political Science
L Education
M Music

N	Fine Arts
P	Language and Literature
Q	Science
R	Medicine
S	Agriculture and Veterinary Science
T	Technology
U	Military Science
V	Naval Science
Z	Books and Libraries, Bibliographies

There is usually more than one letter in a Library of Congress classification, followed by perhaps four numbers and then – in some libraries – by the first three letters of the author's surname. Thus, this book, again on page iv, is classified PN145, meaning:

P	N	145
Language and Literature	Fine arts	Authorship, general works (theory and techniques)

Finally – in the headings to a page of notes – it is always worth recording whence you originally borrowed the book. Some special interest books may not be available from your local library – they may have been searched for, located, and specially borrowed for you by the library. If you can avoid a repeat of the search process this will ease reborrowing. Or you may have borrowed a book from a friend. If you have many friends it will be useful to recall which one possessed it. (And if you are bad at returning borrowed books you will soon have few, if any, friends.)

The notes themselves might take the form of very brief chapter summaries – along the lines of those at the end of each chapter in this book – or merely notes of particular matters of interest. Sometimes you will wish to quote verbatim; at other times you will merely wish to make an *aide memoire.* (But beware: after several years, most *memoires* need a lot of *aide*ing! More comprehensive notes are usually well worth the time they take.)

It is, of course, essential that all notes are accurate; inaccurate notes can be disastrous for a writer. It is also most important for a writer to note precisely where the material he found interesting was located in the book. It is often wise – although not always possible – to refer back to the original when writing. At the least, it is important to be able to relocate your source if you are challenged at some later date. My own practice is to mark book page numbers in the margin of my note sheets.

Cramped notes are almost worthless – in years to come they may not be readable. It is far better to allow plenty of space around all notes. Figure 2.2 shows a page of notes that might be made from a relevant chapter in one of my other books. Note the use of open space; this not only makes the page look more pleasant and easy to read, but it also provides space for later annotation. It is sometimes useful to write notes on alternate halves of the note sheet; plenty of headings and sub-headings are also helpful 'signposts'. A final note of your opinion of the book and its possible appeal to different readers will be useful later, when explaining to your publisher why your book is better than the competition.

In many technical subjects the diagrammatic illustrations in a book provide an effective summary of part of the text. (Figure 2.1 demonstrates this.) It is often worth making a quick copy of important illustrations – or photocopying the few individual pages containing them. And, as in the case of all notes, record in detail the source of the copied illustration, (particularly page number and edition) against the possibility of your wishing at some time in the future to seek permission to reproduce it.

Storage, filing and retrieval

It will have become obvious from the earlier part of this chapter that the research for a book can take a long time. It

---

HOW TO COMMUNICATE

Gordon Wells Pub: McGraw-Hill Book Co (UK) Ltd London 1978
ISBN 0–07–084520–4 Dewey: 658. 4'5 L of C: HF 5718 Own book

Chapter 2 – Principles of Writing

p 12	Basic KISS rule (Keep It Short & Simple)	Alternatively: 4Cs Concise/Clear Complete/Correct
p 13	Short – short words. . . . . short sentences. . . . . short paragraphs.	Avoid four-syllable words Target 15 average 25 max Target 60–80 average 160 max *Note*: short sentences = urgency
	Simple– simple words = short = well-known – use several short and simple words to avoid one difficult (eg four-syllable) one – avoid slang, jargon, buzz-words – always strive for clarity	
p 22	– 'Don't write words or phrases that you would find troublesome to say out loud.'	Simple punctuation too: – comma and full-stop good basis – use only when necessary
p 14	Hard work to write short simple statements	
p 15	Important to identify (and KNOW) your reader	
p 18		*Framework* Organise your writing Separate facts from opinions Model framework for report: Intro. Terms of ref: Background information Facts Opinions Conclusions Recommendations AND A SUMMARY (? at beginning?)
p 24	Be accurate	
p 25	On completion of writing: CHECK	

Fig 2.2 A page of notes based on one chapter in one of my own books – also of interest to many writers.

is a part of the learning process by which you became, or will become, an expert in your field. Perhaps therefore it would have been helpful if you had been able to read this chapter some while ago. (As in, 'If I were wanting to go *there*, I wouldn't be starting from *here*.') That impossibility apart, your researches will, over time, have resulted in a vast amount of information on paper.

This collection of information is fine. A pile of papers in a cardboard box is of little use though; information needs to be organised. The 'ordinary interested reader' may not need to be well organised – the writer does. He needs to be able to *retrieve* stored information at will. And the first step towards organisation might perhaps be the simple one of standardising your borrowed-book notes on to A4 paper, punched with two holes for filing. There is of course nothing sacrosanct about the A4 size, but most photocopies, many magazines and probably your typing paper will be that size anyway, so why not adopt it? (I buy Jumbo pads of the lined, hole-punched A4 paper that is sold in multiple stationers for student use – which means that it is marketed down to as low a price as possible.)

One way of keeping your collected information safely – and tidily – is merely to file it all in big lever-arch files. Punch holes in photocopies and in pages torn from magazines (tear sheets) and file them together with book-notes and any other sheets of notes. Paste small cuttings on to hole-punched A4 sheets and file these too.

But safety and tidiness are not enough. Picture yourself leafing through file after file, each containing perhaps five hundred sheets of useful paper. One simple solution is to give each sheet of paper a number – prefixed by a file letter – and list the contents of each page on a single sheet at the front of each file. This system can be extended to become a better and extremely efficient one by substituting a card-index for the simple contents page.

Thus, the notes on the principles of writing shown as

figure 2.2 might be page number 256 in file B. A totally dissociated photocopy of a magazine article about photographic slides for accompanying talks might be next, on page B257. A 3 inch by 5 inch index card headed (Writing) Techniques, filed under T, would have, as one line of several:

Notes on Wells G 'Principles of Writing' (Techniques) B256

And because of its importance, I would be inclined to cross-index sheet B256 under K for Kiss rule. Sheet B257 would be indexed under V for Visual Aids. When writing, working from a variety of filed sheets, these can easily be extracted from the files, brought together, arranged in sequence, referred to and then – thanks to their unique file numbers – replaced in correct file sequence.

The use of the card-index permits cross-references to many disparate data sources. Important sections in your own books can be indexed on the cards. So too can important articles in journals preserved intact and correspondence filed separately from the research material. It is a very good and extremely flexible system, and I commend it to anyone just starting. It is not the one I use.

I prefer a looser, less tidy, more segregated system of filing. I have either a cardboard document wallet, a large box-file, or a cheap cardboard file for every aspect – or collection of aspects – of every subject in which I am interested. (And sometimes my storage space is merely a large old used envelope, separating papers in a bulging box-file.) Everything I collect goes into the appropriate storage space and I arrange and re-arrange papers in different sequences as I draw on them for my writing. It requires a lot of containers – I already have the equivalent of six filing-cabinet drawers, and need more – but it is extremely flexible. And I can quickly review all the papers I have on any subject without hunting out individual documents from a random store. The number of papers on a small part of a subject is unlikely to be large.

I still find use for a card-index system, but mainly for short notes that do not merit a whole A4 page. Each note is on a separate card, with the subject identified at the top; each card is then merely filed in alphabetical subject order.

I would willingly admit that my system is less well-organised than the undoubtedly better card-index-based one, but I am more interested in writing than in filing. Develop your own filing and retrieval system based on either of the above methods – or on neither. But do not – as is all too easy – let the filing become an end in itself. Your objective is to know about your subject in order to write a book – NOT to have the world's best filing system.

Summary

(1) The fundamental role of a non-fiction book is to communicate accurate factual information. The non-fiction writer is therefore someone who necessarily collects information – a lengthy and continuing process – and who writes about what he knows.

(2) Examination syllabuses are an essential research field for academic textbook writers; the core elements of all relevant syllabuses should be covered, plus complete coverage of as many relevant syllabuses as possible. Coverage and sales go hand-in-hand. Technical book writers also should check all relevant syllabuses and then provide full textual coverage of all, or a specific part of, the syllabuses whenever possible.

(3) Copyright can be infringed if a writer quotes, verbatim, more than about forty or fifty words from another's work without prior permission. A lengthy paraphrase too can be considered plagiarism. Beware – and if in doubt, ask permission.

(4) Research sources include personal experience (and who better than you to write up that most valuable material?),

extended by questionnaires, interviews and correspondence. All other sources are literary – newspaper cuttings, magazine articles, papers in learned journals, and books. Take photocopies whenever possible – with single copies for personal use, the possibility of copyright infringement is slight.

(5) When reading borrowed books, make detailed notes. And, essential for a writer, record full details of the book: title, author, publisher and date, supplemented by ISBN, Dewey and/or Library of Congress classification, and where borrowed from.

(6) Use space lavishly when writing notes, and record book page against all quotations and paraphrases. Preferably prepare notes on hole-punched A4 paper for ease of filing.

(7) Store research material carefully and tidily – either referenced with a card-index or in a multitude of separate document wallets. But beware of having a first-class filing system, the upkeep of which leaves no time for writing. The name of the game is writing, not filing.

3

Developing the idea

The writer of a non-fiction book cannot afford to withdraw from the world and scribble away in an attic. He needs to be something of a salesman. (And see also chapter 10 for advice on the role and use of agents.) Just as an inventor needs to sell his idea to a manufacturer before it can reach the public, so too must a writer sell his idea for a book to a publisher. And the book itself must be directed at a realistic market in which, in turn, the publisher can sell.

So far, in investigating the professional approach to non-fiction writing, we have thought of an idea for a book and have started researching its content. (Depending on the type of book, more or less research will have been completed before contemplating the selling of the idea.) Anyway, it is not yet time to start writing the book.

The professional approach encapsulated in figure 1.1 requires more preparation yet if we are to avoid being left with an unpublished masterpiece. We have to develop a 'sales package'. This is almost an advertising campaign in miniature, directed at publishers, with the objective of persuading them to consider your idea seriously. We must demonstrate that we have thought the idea through and that it has the makings of an interesting book with good sales potential.

The writer's 'sales package' can be thought of as consisting of:

- a detailed description of the 'target reader' – *who* the book is intended to inform

- a detailed description of the book, a chapter-by-chapter synopsis and a good title – *what* the book will include
- a statement of the objectives of the book – *why* there is a need for this particular book and *why* you are the best person to write it.

And the writer's concept of the target reader is both the paramount prerequisite and the continuing essential of a successful book. The lack of such a concept leads to a book that will not be purchased, because no-one can identify himself as in need of it. Figure 3.1 is a check-list of 'sales package' content.

The target reader

It is in the approach to the reader that the professional attitude is most sharply differentiated from that of the amateur writer. The amateur writes what he himself would wish to read, what pleases him as he writes; the professional writes what the reader wants. But this is easily stated, yet could be no more than a platitude. How does the professional write for the reader? Basically, he writes in language that his reader can understand, without being patronising. (And see also chapter 6 for advice on simple writing.) He explains terms or facts that the reader would not be aware of, but not those he knows well.

As an example: the professional writer would, perhaps, not refer to statistical significance in a textbook for middle-school children. But he might say something like, 'The size of the experimental findings was such that the result would probably be similar on future occasions.' In an undergraduate history text he might simply refer to 'the Cade revolt of 1450'. In a middle-school book however, he would at least explain, 'In 1450 the people of Kent and Sussex rose in revolt against the unscrupulous advisers of pious King Henry VI. They were led by Jack Cade who was thought to have been illegitimately related to the House of York.'

1 Have you chosen a short and catchy, yet descriptive, title?

2 Have you clearly identified the target reader? And remembered the special needs of the overseas reader?

3 Have you explained why the reader needs your book and how he will benefit from it?

4 Have you explained why you are well qualified to write the book?

5 Have you described your proposed book in the best possible terms? (Have you presented a good product image?)

6 Does your synopsis demonstrate the major contents of each chapter, and of the book as a whole?

7 Does the synopsis contain sufficient subject matter for a book – but not too much? (You are not writing a trilogy.)

8 Have you covered the whole of the subject, or should you reduce the stated scope to match the coverage?

9 Have you made clear that the book will meet all the requirements of the appropriate and specified examination syllabuses?

10 Have you mentioned competitive books – and explained why yours will be better, or at least a valuable alternative?

Fig 3.1 A check list for the 'sales package' – the statement of objectives and synopsis.

To write at just the right level, in just the right tone for the reader means identifying that reader very clearly. This is most readily done by describing him in some detail. Figure 3.2 illustrates the importance of the target reader concept in developing the writer's sales package. In some cases, depending on the type of book, describing the target reader may entail

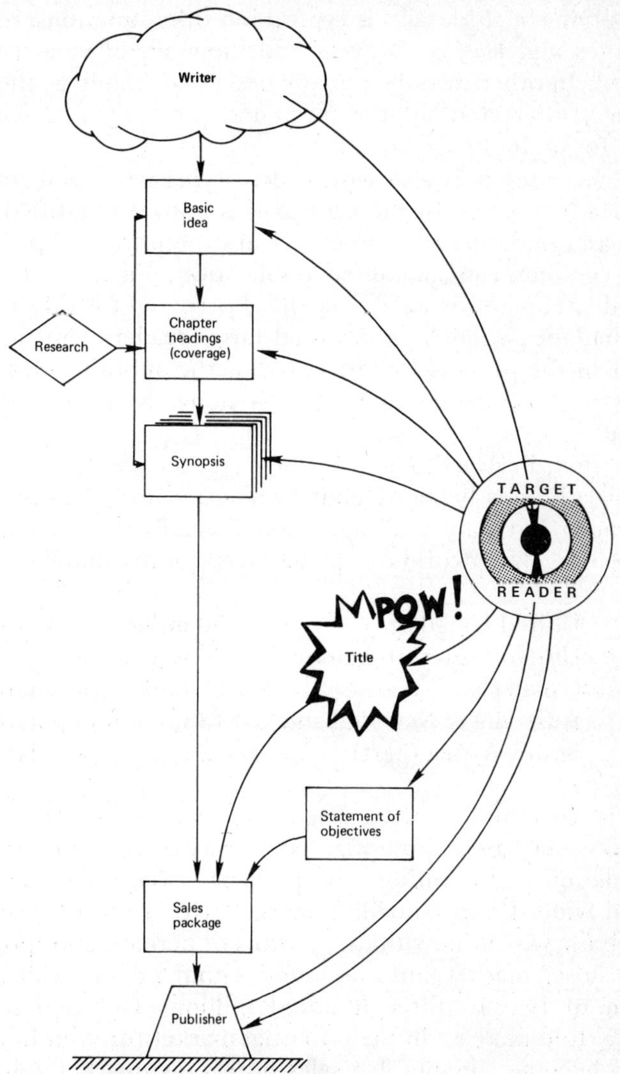

Fig 3.2 The role of the target reader in developing the writer's 'sales package'.

identifying such details as typical job title, functions, responsibilities and age, or the year and the grade at what type of school. In other cases he may be described simply as the keen walker, interested in 'the birds and the bees' and what to look for under hedge bottoms.

In all cases it is also worth identifying what you think is the reader's *need*. In the case of this book I identified *your* need as a guarantee of competence in structuring and presentation; no-one can guarantee publication. Figure 3.3 is the actual statement of objectives that I prepared for this book – and includes a much abbreviated target reader identification. Later in the process I had to provide the publisher with a far more detailed reader-description – along the lines explained above.

At first, in describing your target reader you will probably visualise him as being of your own nationality. This is understandable but parochial, and should usually be resisted. The English-speaking world comprises, very approximately:

United Kingdom	50 million population
United States of America	180 million population
Canada	20 million population
Australia & New Zealand	13 million population
South Africa (part)	2 million population.

Add to that the often English-speaking elite of the third world – perhaps a potential one or two per cent of their population – amounting to perhaps twenty-five million, world wide. From a possible market within the fifty million in Britain, we can now think in terms of perhaps a proportionately lesser market, but one found within a world-wide population of two to three hundred million. This represents a several-fold increase in the potential market for your book.

To become 'eligible' for sales in this vast market you must think of the needs of the overseas reader. How, and to what extent, this advice is taken, is a matter for consideration. Is the book you are proposing to write likely to be of interest to the Asian or African reader? A book on elementary traffic engineering might well be of interest to him; a book on walking and camping in Wales is unlikely to be so. If the book is a fairly basic text it may have potential for overseas sales – and it then pays the writer to keep the overseas reader very much in his mind when writing. Make sure that you include a few extra words of explanation where there is a possibility that the overseas reader may not appreciate a purely local reference.

As an example, around forty per cent of all copies of my own *Traffic Engineering* are sold outside the United Kingdom. In that book I introduced an explanation of the operation of parking meters with the phrase, 'Meters, for those fortunate people who are unfamiliar with them, are . . . '. And the boost to my *ego* when I am confronted by an overseas engineer saying that he started learning traffic engineering from my book is by no means unpleasant.

The target reader, be he British, or living overseas, or an amalgam of both, must always be uppermost in the writer's mind. And he can be very helpful. The writer can repeatedly ask himself, 'Would Abdul Helena McChang understand that?' If the answer is no, the passage should be rewritten.

There will be instances when, although the main bulk of the book is written at the appropriate level for 'AHMcC', more complicated or sophisticated material would be of use to some of the other readers. This problem can be solved by writing the main text for the target reader, with the more sophisticated material appended – out of the main stream. These 'off-line' additions can be in the form of tabulated detailed material, merely summarised in the text; of technical appendixes at the rear of the book; or – the method I prefer and have used effectively – of short, more technical, inserts in the text itself, but segregated within 'boxes'. It is also possible to incorporate off-line material in footnotes but this is not recommended. It is more difficult for the printer, and therefore expensive, and it does not look attractive. (And there is no doubt that footnotes put off the non-academic reader.)

The synopsis

Having a clear idea of what the book is to be about, a knowledge of how much of the subject is to be dealt with, and at what educational and interest level it is to be directed, we now need to think more about the content. And the first essential is to *think book.*

What is a book? Let us define it as consisting of about fifty thousand words, divided into more-or-less self-contained chapters – and the commercial reasons behind this length are explained further in chapter 5. Commonly, a fifty-thousand-word general non-fiction book is divided into around ten or twelve chapters, obviously averaging four to five thousand words per chapter. (There is nothing 'wrong' with twenty chapters each of two thousand five hundred words – but longer chapters are more normal. There is also the question of appearance; four thousand words will be about ten printed pages, five sheets of paper. Shorter chapters give the impression that the writer didn't really get started – or worse, that he didn't know much about that part of the subject.)

Set down on a sheet of paper the separate parts of your subject. At this stage, don't trouble with logic or sequence – just divide up the whole into self-contained bits. Every subject can be sub-divided; if you have not already done so, now is the time to do it. My initial thoughts about this book – my 'doodles' – in random order, were:

- attitude of mind – professionalism (basically, don't write until the idea is sold)
- the basic idea – who will read it? (the target reader)
- selling the idea – approaching publishers – don't give up easily, there are lots of publishers

- production and publicity – help the publisher to sell your book
- business matters – royalties, agreements, tax
- writing – write to budget: accuracy, brevity, clarity
- illustrations – page-size limitations
- preparing typescript – A4, double-spaced, etc.: make sure it is right at this stage, later is too late
- index preparation – now or later, how I do it
- editing – explain difference between commissioning and copy-editors; check that copy-editor does not accidentally destroy sense
- proofs and proofreading – cost of alterations; list symbols
- next book – and/or second edition
- writer's library – research techniques

The next stages – and they tend to run together – are to rearrange the initial chapter-ideas into a logical sequence and to expand on the contents of each chapter. As you will know by now, I ran together the section on attitude of mind with the section on the basic idea to make the introductory first chapter. I changed the preliminary sequence – my first thoughts – to put business matters at the end – and I am still not sure whether or not that was the best sequence. I split this chapter away from 'selling the idea' because I thought the development of the sales package was important enough to warrant a chapter of its own – and not to have done so would have meant an unevenly long chapter. I separated research from the writer's library and brought it right to the front in a chapter of its own – but thereby left the library idea a bit 'thin'.

There is seldom just one single *correct* sequence, merely different people's opinions. It is, of course, important to ensure that, in order to understand the content of one chapter, the reader is not required to have read a later one. Clearly such a sequence would need changing.

The contents of each chapter need to be listed, but briefly.

The purpose of this synopsis is threefold:

(1) To demonstrate to the publisher that you intend to cover each 'chapter-subject' adequately. (And he may wish to suggest further aspects to be covered, which can only be helpful to the writer – we all overlook something.)
(2) To act as the first check-list of material to be covered by the writer when actually writing.
(3) To give a general 'feel' of the proposed book's contents – for the publisher's sales team and, through them, for potential customers.

The way the synopsis is actually written should be fairly brief while describing the content adequately, and as near to the eventual sequence as possible. The synopsis notes should be fuller than the sub-headings that appear in, for instance, this book's contents page, but not greatly different in their ideas. The synopsis for this chapter of this book read:

> **Developing the idea**: Define target-reader; explain style differences for example junior technician/research student/ undergraduate/layman. Develop major thoughts into logical sequence. 'Think book' = ten chapters, each of 5000 words – explain why. Development of synopsis and title. Importance of title. Book-objective statement – *who* would read the book and why *you* should be the one to write it.

A warning though. Do not become too firmly committed to your synopsis. At this stage it must be thought of as a draft. The publisher who accepts your sales package may wish to expand it, to contract it, or to change its sequence. And it is usually wise to go along with such publisher's suggestions; they will be intended to improve the book and its sales potential – and anyway, he's paying, or will be.

There may be aspects of the subject that do not justify a chapter to themselves. The first solution, of course, is to incorporate such aspects into another appropriate chapter – as I did here, in bringing together the thoughts about professionalism and the need to choose a basic subject. Neither of these seemed to me to warrant a full-length chapter, but they fitted well together as chapter 1. Inevitably though, some aspects of a subject are unavoidably free-standing, yet are too small for a chapter. Such a subject is the writer's library – about which I have something useful to say, but not a lot. As you will see, I am treating this as an appendix – not because it is too technical (see above) but because, in my view, it does not easily fit in anywhere else.

The title

I find that ideas for a title often come to me whilst developing the synopsis. This is convenient, for the title is an essential part of the sales package. It is the writer's equivalent of the big, star-burst-surrounded, phrase that attracts the shoppers – 'Special Discount Offer' or 'Beat the Budget – Buy Now'. And, like the supermarket sales-pitch, it is most effective if brief and catchy.

The purpose of a book-title is to attract (favourable) attention, to identify the book and, persuasively, to describe its content. And, today, it must be brief. A title such as 'A Manual of Conceptual Design Standards and Policies for Widget Technicians', which might – if it were not a product of my imagination – have been acceptable fifty years ago, would not be so today. Not only does it look old-fashioned; it is too long to be easily referred to, or to have any sales impact at all, and – of considerable technical production importance – it would not fit across the top of each alternate page of the book. The printer would also find it troublesome to print all that on the spine of the book – which, at fifty thousand words, is relatively thin. Sub-titles can supplement a short title, but they too are no longer favoured, unless they are the only way of adequately describing the book.

The title at which to aim is one of no more than three or four words. In most of my books I have so far succeeded in keeping to that target, while clearly defining the subject of each book. And if you cannot define, clearly and concisely, what your book is about, perhaps the subject itself is less clear or self-contained than you thought?

To start you thinking of suitable titles, ask questions of yourself:

(1) *What will the book help the reader to do*? Hence 'How to Widget', 'Profit from Your Widget', or 'Widgeting for Beginners'.
(2) *What is the conventional title of the subject*? Can you call your book 'Widgetary Simplified', 'Simple Widgetary', or better, 'Successful Widgetary'?
(3) *What do you think of yourself as*? This might lead to such a title as 'The Successful Widgeter' – or even 'The Compleat Widget'.

Notice the use of such descriptive, yet persuasive, phrases as 'How to . . . ', 'Successful . . . ', 'Profit from . . . '. In each case they are suggesting that buying your book will enable the reader to do something previously beyond him, to succeed, to make money, or to start on a new occupation or hobby.

Notice also that the subject is made crystal clear by the title. There is no room in non-fiction titling for the erudite allusion or the partial quotation. (I dream of a book on brewing techniques entitled 'The Precious Half', alluding to the delightful line in Fitzgeralds's *Rubaiyat of Omar Khayyam*, 'I often wonder what the Vintners buy One half so precious as the Goods they sell' – which I know only because it is painted on the wall of a favourite hostelry.)

The statement of objectives

The purpose of the statement of a proposed book's objectives is to convey to the publisher much of the thinking that we have already discussed in this chapter. The statement of objectives is the 'hard sell' document, pointing out to the publisher why he should consider your idea and your synopsis. With luck your title has already caught a publisher's eye; the self-inflicted questions which helped to produce that title are again relevant.

The statement of objectives needs to show:

- Who will buy the book – that is, the target-reader.
- What the book will help the reader to do; how it will help him to do something better.
- Why the target reader needs knowledge or instruction in the book's subject.
- Which (general) position at work the book will help the reader to approach or aspire to (e.g. 'become a managing director' or 'become a foreman widgeter'.)
- Why you are ideally qualified to write this book.
- How thoroughly the book covers which examination syllabuses.
- What competitive books are on the market and why you think that your book can carve out a portion of the market.

Fortuitously, much of the work that you will put into writing this statement is of further use. Both the preface – where a book has one – and the inevitable blurb, usually on the jacket or back cover of the book, should incorporate much of its content. (All three – statement of objectives, preface and blurb – serve the same basic purpose, to explain why the book is worth buying.)

Figure 3.3 is the statement of objectives that I prepared for this book. It demonstrates most of the points in the above list. Notice how the opening paragraph identifies the target reader very specifically, while at the same time suggesting the possibility of a wider market. And its limitations – not

THE SUCCESSFUL AUTHOR'S HANDBOOK Gordon Wells

This book is directed at the potential writer of a specialist or professional book or textbook. It is meant for the specialist in almost any field, from office mailroom layout to nursing, from gardening to widget manufacturing, who wants to write a book about it. It will, however, be equally appropriate for intending writers of other types of non-fiction books. The principles could as well be applied by a biographer, or by the person wanting to write a travel book, as by the specialist. It will not help anyone to write a book of fiction.

This book will not guarantee that the reader/writer who follows its advice will produce a best-seller, or even just a saleable book. There may be no market for a book on an esoteric subject, no matter how dear it may be to the writer's heart. (After reading the book, however, he may understand better why he hasn't been able to get his own book published.) This book *will* guarantee that if a writer follows the advice contained in it, his own book will be well-structured and professionally presented: the content remains his own responsibility.

There is always room for another good book on most subjects. There are hundreds of publishers in Britain, each producing numbers of new books each year. In all, something like thirty thousand new books are published in Britain each year. Eighty per cent of these are non-fiction titles. Many of these are by first-time writers, who need to learn their writing trade. This book will set them right: it will show them how to be a successful author.

Fig 3.3 An example of a statement of objectives – for this book.

fiction – are made immediately clear. The second paragraph explains what the book is intended to do for you, while the third paragraph explains briefly why the reader *needs* the book. The explanation of the need for this particular book is less necessary than usual. Publishers know better than anyone

Writing is a satisfying occupation. But a writer will not only be 'fulfilled' by getting into print: there are other benefits. Royalties will vary according to the type of book. A book of narrow specialist interest and selling at a high price will naturally earn less money for the writer than a medium-priced general interest book or a cheap, bulk-selling text book. But there will always be some money. The writer will also gain professional kudos from any book. His professional career will probably benefit even from a low-selling book. (Or even more so in some circles.) This book will help anyone to start on the road to successful authorship. It will also be a helpful guide to the unintentional writer – the expert approached, out of the blue, by a publisher with the offer of a commission to write a book on his speciality.

I am well qualified to write this book having written several specialist engineering textbooks, several children's books explaining technical subjects in a simple way and three general non-fiction books. I attach a list of my published books. Reviewers have frequently commented on my ability to explain complex matters in a simple way.

The only other book covering a similar field, but slanted much more towards the general interest non-fiction writer, is: David St John Thomas: *Non-Fiction*, David & Charles, Newton Abbot, 1970 (OP). Most books for writers deal with fiction writing. There are several such books but they should not be in competition with the proposed book.

Gordon Wells

how much the specialist needs to be advised on how to set about writing his book. Note also the hint of the title at the end of the third paragraph.

The fourth paragraph is perhaps a bit of 'padding'. A publisher does not need to be told this, but I thought it worth including, to bring in the point about professional kudos. The paragraph serves effectively the same purpose as one explaining how another book will help the reader better himself at his job. Again, I hinted at the title at the end, to emphasise it.

The fifth paragraph is meant to be a careful balance between telling the publisher what a fine fellow I am, and preserving my accustomed modesty. If I did not explain that I was already a successful writer the publisher would rightly ask what qualifications I had to write this particular book. The sixth paragraph merely refers to the only directly competitive book that I knew of at the time.

As you know, because this *is* the book, my sales package was successful (And I hope that you, my target reader, will benefit from it as I expect.) In the next chapter we will look at the selling process itself.

Summary

(1) Before starting to write, a non-fiction writer should sell his idea to a publisher. This is best done with a 'sales package' explaining:
who the book is for;
what the book is about;
why there is a need for it; and
why it should be written by you.

(2) The target reader should not be restricted to the home market – remember the rest of the English-speaking world. The concept of the target reader should be in the forefront of the writer's mind the whole time he is writing – 'Will Abdul Helena McChang understand that?'

(3) The chapters of a book should follow a logical sequence. Each chapter should, as far as possible, fully cover its own part of a subject, while being of a reasonable length. (A normal minimum chapter length of about four thousand words is recommended.)

(4) The synopsis should demonstrate to the publisher that each part of a subject is adequately covered, and in an internally logical sequence.

(5) A brief, catchy, yet descriptive title is essential. Without it the book will sell less well – to both the publisher and, eventually, to the public. Brevity is particularly necessary for printing the title across page headings.

(6) The statement of objectives draws together the details of the target reader and *his* need for *your* book. It is the 'hard sell' part of the sales package.

4
Selling the idea

We now have something to sell – the 'sales package', comprising a detailed description of the book we are proposing and a description of the likely market for that book. The market for the 'sales package' itself is different. It can only be sold once, to a publisher, but which one?

Publishers are legion; not all of them will be interested in the sort of book you intend to write. Your first task is to find the publishers that *might* be interested; then from that list, the one that *is* interested. The first step in listing potential publishers is probably to check who published the other books on the same general subject. If your book is not in direct competition with one of their books they may be interested. (And in some cases, even if your book will be competing with one of theirs, they might still be interested.)

Listing publishers

Start by listing the publishers of the books on your own shelves. Extend this list by looking in bookshops and libraries for books on the same general subject. With many specialist subjects the resultant list will not be very long. Do not overlook the smaller, often fairly specialist publishers; not every good book is published by the giants. But, conversely, do not be shy of including the giants in your list; they are just as keen to attract good new books by new writers as are the smaller publishers.

The annual *Writers' & Artists' Yearbook* (A & C Black) is a further, invaluable, source of suitable publishers. The *Yearbook* lists virtually all the book publishers in the United Kingdom, giving the postal address, the names of directors and, in most cases, detailing the broad areas in which each publisher specialises. For example, the Macmillan Press entry lists areas of interest as:

> College, Academic, Scientific and Technical Works, publishers of Grove's Dictionary of Music and Musicians, and the Stateman's Year-Book, and other Reference Works.

This is unhelpfully broad. Since I wrote this book, however, there is another handbook which offers more assistance, albeit about many fewer publishers, than does the *Writers' & Artists' Yearbook*. This is my own *The Book Writer's Handbook* (Allison & Busby/W.H. Allen, 1989), which includes up-to-date examples of the types of books each publisher (currently) welcomes.

At this stage too – while listing suitable publishers to whom you might offer your book idea – it is useful to study these publishers' catalogues. The catalogues will tell you more about their books in the same general area as yours. You may be able to discern an underlying pattern in their books which would preclude or ideally fit together with yours. Look also for book series into which yours – perhaps amended – might fit.

Sort your list of publishers into some kind of order. It is obviously sensible to start with the one you think most likely to be just waiting for your book. (Or perhaps start with the publisher you would most *like* to be published by, which is not necessarily the same thing.)

Approaching publishers

You are now ready to write to publisher number one. Yes, even if you live just around the corner from the publisher's office, write to him. You are trying to sell him your idea for a book; books consist of written words. The publisher is going to be interested – if at all – only in your written work. You may have the most sexy or manly (or both?) voice imaginable, but do not telephone the publisher to tell him about your book idea. And even if you are Miss or Mister Universe, do not call in person. Your voice or figure may perhaps be enjoyed, but will undoubtedly be deflected by a receptionist; your letter with its sales package will reach the desk of someone on the editorial staff.

Your letter, and the complete sales package as described in chapter 3, will of course be typed. I suppose a publisher might not damn your work immediately if the letter was handwritten, but you are trying to act professionally in a commercial world where almost everything is typed. So, if you cannot – yet – type yourself, persuade, or pay, someone to type for you. Without doubt the sales package *must* be typed; that is going to be read in some detail by many people. If they find difficulty in deciphering your handwriting you are starting off with a major disadvantage – assuming anyone bothers to attempt to read it.

My practice is to type the sales package – usually one sheet for the statement of objectives and one or two for the synopsis – and then to make three or four photocopies of it. I send a photocopy only to the publishers, with, obviously, an original letter in each case. Do not get too enthusiastic about photocopying though, and never submit the proposal to more than one publisher at a time. You are offering a single idea; as in marriage, attempts at polygamy usually cause universal rejection.

The letter accompanying the sales package can be brief; everything important is in the sales package. I would say something like:

Dear Sir,

I am writing to enquire whether or not you might be interested in a new book about Widgetology, intended to meet the need for a college text in that subject.

I enclose a brief statement of the objectives of my proposed book 'You and the Widget', together with my qualifications for writing such a book, and a synopsis of the proposed contents. I would, of course, be prepared to amend the synopsis to meet your requirements should you be interested.

I enclose a stamped addressed envelope for your reply.

Yours faithfully

Gordon Wells

Notice the final paragraph in the covering letter; the reply-paid envelope. You want a reply from the publisher; the stamped envelope virtually guarantees that you get one. Suppose a publisher receives thirty to forty unsolicited book ideas a week – only one or two of which are worth taking further – his postage bill, without likelihood of profit, will soon mount up. A small sum, yes, but remember that old saw about looking after the pennies.

The letter and sales package despatched, forget them – if you can. Concentrate on research if possible, or do those household repairs that have been left while you worked on the synopsis. Whatever you do, do not telephone the publisher to check that he received the letter; the postal service really is remarkably reliable – he got it. Just wait. You may get a reply within a week or so saying 'no.' The publisher may not reply for a couple of months – and still say 'no'. I sometimes delude myself that a delayed reply means that the publisher is giving the idea more and more thought. This may be so – but it can just as easily mean that the editor who is considering your suggestion has many synopses on his desk, and yours is not yet at the top of the heap. If you do not get any reply within two months, you can try a polite 'chaser'.

Rejection

The rejection of your synopsis can be short and to the point, or apologetically encouraging. Being human, I am always encouraged by encouragement. I prefer the 'what a good idea but we are fully committed' ones, or even better, the 'I wish we could take it but we are full up: try Blank's, they are just starting a new series that this looks ideal for,' ones. I had one of these 'try Blank's' rejection letters once. I tried Blank's and they gave me a contract within weeks. (More about contracts in chapter 10.)

But short or encouraging, a rejection is a rejection is a rejection. A rejection can never be what you *want* but you must never be put off by it. It is said that when George Bernard Shaw started writing articles, he collected enough rejection slips to paper a room. (When an article is rejected all you get is a small printed rejection slip; at least with a book synopsis you usually get a personal letter.) My idea for *How to Communicate* was rejected by twelve publishers before McGraw-Hill persuaded me to broaden its scope and make it into a commercial proposition. (If McGraws had rejected the idea I still had a list of a dozen more publishers to try.)

As soon as you receive a rejection letter, resubmit the sales package to the number two publisher on your list. And if he rejects it, resubmit to number three, and so on. Apart from helping you to survive the rejection pains, it keeps the idea out 'on offer'.

If you get several rapid rejections, stop and think again. Possible reasons for rejection include:

- the idea is lousy – *is* it?
- the package does not present the idea well – does it not?
- all the publishers are over-stocked for their future programmes.
- all the publishers are stupid or blind – that is, everyone is 'out of step' except you. No. Most publishers are astute business men, or they would go out of business. But they *are* capable of making errors of judgement.
- there are already enough books on the market on the subject – what about your market research?
- there is no market for the idea – *is* it too esoteric?
- you are trying the wrong publishers – quite likely.

Assuming that after your rethink you remain convinced that the idea is worth proceeding with, that there *is* a market for it, and that the sales package presents the idea as well as possible, off you go again. (And do not be put off by advice that another book on the same subject is being prepared by someone else. It is unlikely that you will both cover exactly the same ground.) Submit the sales package to the next publisher in your list. Personally, if I were convinced that a book idea was good, I would not give up until I had tried at least twenty well-chosen publishers. And even then, I would probably assume that the general economic state of the nation had influenced the publishers' views. In a couple of years' time I would cautiously try out the idea again, on a very few selected publishers.

But let us not assume the worst. One of your selected list of publishers shows interest. You may get a telephone call or you may get a letter. You may be invited to call and discuss the idea further, or you may be asked to submit a few sample chapters. Figure 4.1 shows, in flow chart format, the process from now on.

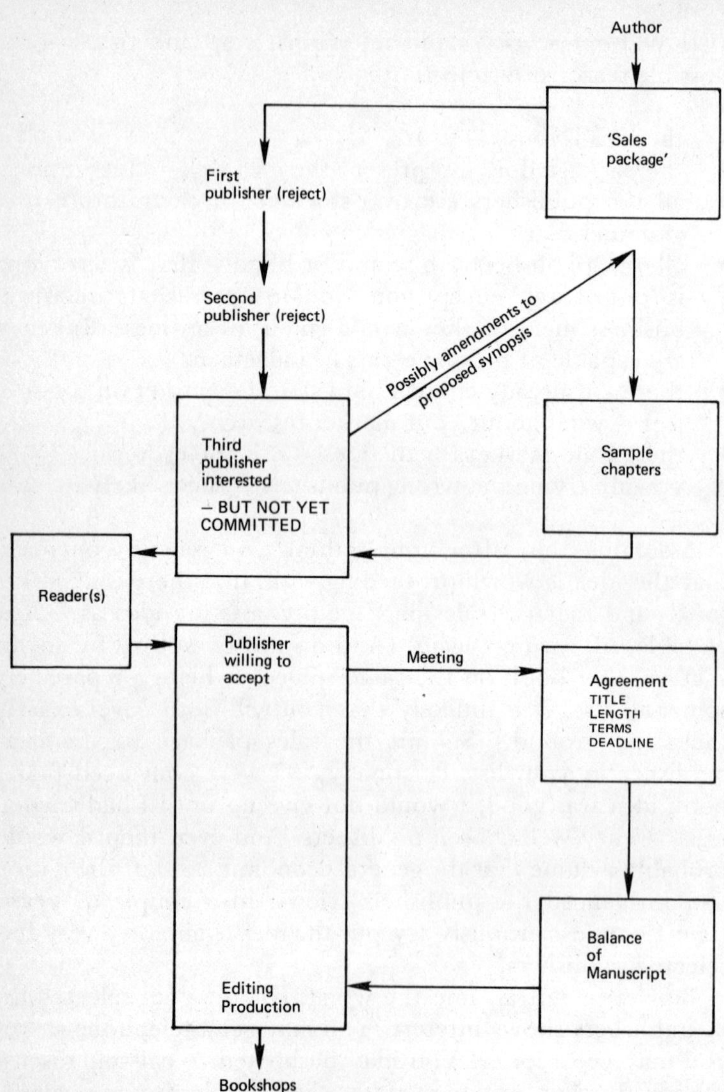

Fig 4.1 A flow chart of the process from the preparation of the 'sales package' to the delivery of the manuscript to the publisher.

Meeting the publisher

Your first contact with a publisher is likely to be with a sponsoring or commissioning editor (or some such title) who will have expressed some interest in your idea. He or she may think that your idea is just what they have been waiting for; or more likely, that suitably amended, it might be made to fit their requirements. The commissioning editor will have to justify taking on your book; he will have to convince a more senior editor and/or an editorial board. He needs to convince himself first. Once committed, the commissioning editor will be personally involved with your book.

As you progress, you may lean heavily on your editor; a good one will feed you with extra ideas, lend you relevant source material, open otherwise-closed doors, and generally offer a sympathetic ear. A good working relationship with a sympathetic editor is a 'rich and wondrous thing' for a writer.

Sponsoring editors can be male or female. I tend to refer to them as 'he'; this is not chauvinism, it is laziness. I like lady editors, but 'he' requires one less stroke on the typewriter than does 'she'. Liberated lady readers please note, read 'she' for 'he', and do not write to complain!

At your first meeting, the editor will probably make suggestions for improving the synopsis; extend the scope here, add in a chapter about this, run those two 'thin' chapters together. (For commercial reasons, Macmillans asked me to reduce the length of this book from my planned 50 000 words to just over 40 000. I complied.) Whatever the suggestions, consider them carefully. Discuss the reasons for them and be prepared to accommodate them. The editor sees many more books, across a far wider field, than you, and will have a better idea of market needs and saleability than you. The suggestions will usually make good commercial sense and should usually be adopted. An editor will seldom know a great deal about your specialist field. He will certainly know more about publishing than you.

I have always found it very useful to make quick rough notes during such initial meetings – I do not rely on my memory. As soon as I leave the meeting, I write up my notes – recording such things as my promises of providing material or making changes, and deadlines agreed. If I think it would be useful, I confirm promises and dates in writing to the editor that evening.

The sample chapters

The culmination of a meeting with the publisher may be a requirement for a rewritten synopsis. More likely, the requirement will be for that plus samples of your work. In the case of the 'average' general non-fiction book of fifty thousand words in ten to twelve chapters, the requirement might be for a couple of chapters. Some college or academic texts may comprise a large number of smaller sections, geared to individual work-sessions, within a possibly longer book; in such cases, and as a more general rule, the sample requirement would be for about twenty per cent of the eventual whole. These sample chapters must be complete; if the final book is to have illustrations, chapter summaries, and end-of-chapter examples, so too should the samples.

Now at last, you can start writing. The next few chapters of this book deal, at some length, with the mechanics and the process of writing. It is sufficient in this chapter to point out that you, and the whole of your book, will be judged on the quality of the sample chapters. Make them really good ones. If you sweat at your writing, sweat buckets over these sample chapters; if they do not 'sell', neither will the book. (And if you suffer from the delusion that good writing comes easy, forget it; it is hard work.)

Do not keep the publisher waiting too long for the sample chapters either; strike back while the editor's memory is still fresh and receptive. If you know your subject well, you should be able to draft, revise and type eight to ten thousand words within at most three or four weeks. Obviously, unless the editor specifies the chapters he wants for the sample, you will choose to write those chapters dealing with aspects of the subject you know best. It is seldom sensible to write the first two chapters as samples.

Type up the sample chapters, exactly as the whole manuscript will be presented, and despatch to the publisher (see chapter 8). And, as with the basic sales package, *post* the sample chapters. If the editor wants to talk about them, he will contact you.

At this stage I prefer to provide photocopies of the sample chapters, and this is quite acceptable for the samples. (Photocopies sometimes smudge and are not suitable for the final typescript from which the printer works.) Using photocopies at this stage permits retention, in good condition, of the originals for eventual complete submission. Another alternative is to submit a carbon copy as the sample chapters together with a request for their return for eventual resubmission.

You can expect an early acknowledgement from the editor – especially if you ask for one and provide a stamped addressed envelope. The editor will have several book ideas 'on the boil'. (Thirty or forty books at various stages in their development, and not all of which will come to fruition, is not an unusual work-load for a commissioning editor.) He will not therefore be giving your sample chapters his immediate and undivided attention. What does he do with them?

After reading through the sample chapters and the revised synopsis himself, to ensure that they are intelligible and reasonably up to standard, the editor will send the samples to one or more readers, for review. The readers will be experts in your field. (Your identity will not normally be revealed; nor will that of the readers.) On the comments and opinions of the readers rests – to a large, but thank God not complete, extent – the fate of your proposed book. But readers are sometimes overruled. If the book goes ahead, the readers' comments may be sent to you as helpful suggestions – no more – for improvement.

It is useful for a writer to know the kind of questions that the readers are asked to answer. Figure 4.2 lists typical questions; it is equally useful as a check-list for the writer himself. With technical and specialist non-fiction writing, the grammar, syntax, etc. are of less importance, at this stage, than the content and the logic. Grammatical errors can readily be corrected during copy-editing (see chapter 9.)

Commissioning the book

Assuming that the readers' comments are generally favourable, the editor will think long and hard about the commercial logic of your book. The readers may think it marvellous, but if it will cost a lot to produce, it may price itself out of its market. The editor will make cost estimates or get rough quotations for producing the book and will try to convince himself of the number of copies that will sell at what price. In larger publishing houses he may then need to seek the approval of an editorial board to go ahead with the book. In smaller firms he may make the final decision himself.

If the decision of the editor, and if necessary, the editorial board, is to go ahead with your book, a contract – an agreement – will be prepared. The content of a typical publishers' agreement is examined in more detail in chapter 10. In essence, the publisher agrees to publish your book, if up to the standard of the sample, provided that you deliver it to him by an agreed date. (But see chapter 10 for further comments about the acceptability of a commissioned manuscript.) He contracts to pay you royalties – a percentage of the price of the book or of the net receipts – on all sales. Most agreements provide for the payment of an advance on royalties. This may be paid when the agreement is signed, when the manuscript is delivered, or on publication date; some advances are paid half on signing and half on delivery or publication. Advances too are further discussed in chapter 10.

1 Questions about the market

(a) What are the principal books with which this one will have to compete? How does it differ?

(b) To whom, particularly, would this book appeal?

(c) If it is an educational book, at what level? (Degree, diploma, certificate, etc.)

(d) How widely is the subject taught, or of interest?

(e) Is the demand for such a book likely to increase, remain constant, or decline?

2 Questions about content and organisation

(a) Is the treatment authoritative, modern, and technically correct? Is there anything out-of-date or superfluous?

(b) Are there any noticeable omissions in the synopsis or the text?

(c) Is the book well-planned, consecutive chapters developing the subject logically?

(d) Is there effective continuity within each chapter?

(e) Are there sufficient, suitable, examples and exercises in the text?

3 Questions about style and learning aids

(a) Is the writing clear and concise?

(b) Is the writer's style suitable to hold the reader's interest, or is it dull and verbose?

(c) Is the vocabulary at the appropriate educational level for the intended reader?

(d) Are the illustrations sufficient, relevant and functional?

(e) Are check lists appropriate: if so, are there enough suitable ones?

4 The crux question

Do you recommend that we encourage the writer to comlete this book with a view to our publishing it?

Fig 4.2 Some typical questions for a publisher's review of sample chapters. Ask yourself the same questions.

Once you have the signed agreement you can start writing your book in earnest. It means that the publisher and you are in agreement; the publisher intends to publish your book, you intend to write it.

But the agreement is not always as cast-iron and copper-bottomed as some may think. Some writers never complete and deliver the book they have *agreed* to write; publishers do not sue writers for non-delivery. There may be a major economic recession, putting the publisher under unexpected and serious financial strain. He may be compelled to reduce his publishing programme, and not publish your book. Should this happen – most unusual, but it happened to me – a reputable publisher would offer the writer some financial compensation. If the final book manuscript was far below the standard of the sample chapters, and was not capable of being doctored into shape, the publisher might refuse to publish – and would not offer compensation. But, in general terms, your book is now very likely to be published.

Reference has already been made to the date for the completed manuscript to be delivered to the publisher. The editor will have discussed this date with you – and may have pushed you to a tighter deadline than you might wish. Delivery within six months of signing the agreement is about par for a fairly general non-fiction book. This might be cut to three months if the subject matter involved little or no research – a book like this one perhaps. For an academic text the delivery date might well be upwards of a year away.

Remember that when you sign the agreement you are agreeing to the delivery date included in it. If it is quite impracticable, tell the publisher so. If you do not tell him, he will organise his production schedules around that date. If your future non-delivery upsets the production schedules this can both increase its costs and also considerably delay rescheduling your book into the programme.

(In my experience, the production schedules are almost always upset by delays caused by reviewers, or editors, or printers. Your book will probably appear weeks – or months – after the originally intended publication date. But let the delays be the faults of others – *you* are striving to act professionally, to be efficient.)

One consequence of the tight deadlines that publishers will often push writers into – or at least, towards – is the need to know your subject well. You will have to research as you write to check facts, but the writing period in book preparation is no time for woolly, uncertain, thinking. Sort your ideas out before you get into the rat-race, before you sign the agreement.

What if the idea is 'sold' to you?

So far in this book we have been considering the case of the writer with an idea for a book that, if marketable, he eventually persuades a publisher to 'sponsor', to *publish*. Sometimes a book is initiated differently. The need for a particular book may be perceived by a publisher himself. He then seeks out a specialist in that subject and persuades him to write a book about it.

A publisher may be preparing a uniform series of college texts to meet a clutch of new technology syllabuses; he needs a book on widgeting. You are the national expert on widgeting – perhaps even sat on the committee that drafted the widgeting syllabus. By asking around, the publisher is given your name as *the* expert. The publisher's commissioning editor contacts you – initially by letter, but shortly thereafter in person – and discusses the idea of a book. You had never before thought of writing a book – or at least, you will not admit to your thoughts. What do you do?

Really, you are in a similar position to the man with a book-idea to sell – but with the uncertainty partly removed. You are being given a good head start. The publisher *wants* a book on your subject and he wants *you* to write it. All you now have to do is to justify that initial need and faith.

You still need to do much of what has already been described. Specifically you should:

- investigate the competitive texts; the commissioning editor should help with this.
- gear yourself mentally to writing the book; think-through your motivation.
- ensure that you can cover the whole subject – or that you can persuade a colleague to help fill in your gaps.
- study all the relevant examination syllabuses, not just the one(s) you know well.
- define the target-reader – the commissioning editor should help with this too.
- prepare the synopsis, its purpose still being just as explained in chapter 3. Agree it with the editor.
- think about – and perhaps suggest – a title; but the commissioning editor may already have a title in mind that conforms with the rest of the series.
- write sample chapters. Even though you were approached by the publisher, the editor still needs the reassurance that good sample reviews can give him, before he finally gives you a contract. He needs to be sure that you actually can write.

From here on, everything in this book applies equally to the writer who approaches the publisher himself, as to the writer approached by the publisher direct. No matter from which side you approach the writing grindstone, your nose will still be in extended contact with it.

There is one further form of specialist non-fiction writing on which we have not yet touched: the compiling and editing of contributed handbooks. The hopeful editor of a potential handbook can as readily approach a publisher with a handbook idea as can a 'whole-book' writer. In effect he will say, 'There is a need for a book on widgetology. I can persuade these experts to write chapters for it, for me. I will ensure that the final book is a cohesive whole.' Equally, a publisher can often seek out a specialist able to put together a collection of expert contributions in the form of a handbook. The publisher himself will have perceived the need for such a handbook; the publisher needs an advisory editor, respected in the particular profession. The task of the handbook editor is examined further in chapter 6.

Summary

(1) Select several publishers likely to be interested in a book such as you propose. Arrange your list of publishers in order of the likelihood of their accepting the book.

(2) Write – do not call or telephone – to the first publisher, enclosing the 'sales package' of statement of objectives and synopsis. If the first publisher rejects the idea, submit it immediately to the next on the list, and so on.

(3) If you get too many rapid rejections, review your sales package. If still convinced of its worth, carry on submitting it to publishers. If the idea is good, and there is a market for it, there will almost certainly be a publisher somewhere.

(4) Once a publisher shows interest in your idea, his editor may offer suggestions for improving the synopsis – making it a 'better buy'. Consider them carefully; this is the editor's speciality. A wise writer relies on, and works with, not against, his editor.

(5) If (or more likely, when) asked for sample chapters, provide them quickly and make sure that they are the best you can do. (Write the chapters at which you feel most competent – not necessarily the first two.)

(6) Experts in your field will read your sample chapters and synopsis and tell the publisher what they think of them. Their comments, if shown to you, may help in later chapters and/or amendments of the samples. The identity of the reviewers is not usually revealed to you.

(7) If the reviews are good and if the publisher decides that the idea is a commercial proposition, he will offer you a contract to produce the book for him to publish. Only now should you start to write the balance of the book, and work to the publisher's delivery deadline – it is most important that you meet it.

(8) If a publisher approaches you with a request that you write a book for him, you still need to go through many of the processes described so far – target reader identification, synopsis, sample chapters, etc. – but you have the major advantage of being in a seller's market. And the buyer will know what he wants.

5
The mechanics of writing

The idea for the book sold, the time has come for the real work. Now you have to write the rest of the book. And there is a certain amount of overlap in time between the advice that follows and the action already taken in preparing the sample chapters, but of course you will have read this chapter and the next before actually applying the process advised in the previous chapters.

The word-budget

In chapter 3 we looked at the development of the synopsis within a framework leading to a finished book about fifty thousand words long. It is now advisable, if this was not done when preparing the synopsis, to divide up the now agreed number of words between the chapters. Ideally, as already mentioned, each chapter should be about the same length, but we do not live in an ideal world. There will be some chapters that need more words than others and others that cannot really stretch to a standard length.

Work through the synposis assessing the number of words you will need to cover the contents of each chapter. Add together the chapter length assessments to ensure that they still total the necessary book length. Do not just assess the words in the chapters – remember the extras, the preface, the bibliography, the appendixes, all of which are part of the book and need to be included in the word-total. Your assessments will be wrong but they will be the target at which you aim. Together, they are your *word-budget* for the book.

The word-budget is not only a target, it also serves as a disciplinary measure. It ensures that you do not gloss over a less-interesting but equally important part of the subject. We will return to the use of the word-budget as a target later in this chapter. Figure 5.1 shows the word-budget to which I worked in writing this book – and how I lived up to it.

The word-budget is also important because the agreement that you and your publisher have by now signed will specify the book length. If you produce a manuscript of half the agreed length the book may no longer be a commercial proposition. Too long a book may also be disastrous.

Chapter	Target words	Target Running total	Achieved words	Achieved Running total	Illustrations achieved			
					Diagrams*	Textual	Total	Running total
1	3000	3000	2800	2800	0	1	1	1
2	4000	7000	4100	6900	1	1	2	3
3	4000	11000	4000	10900	1	2	3	6
4	4000	15000	4500	15400	1	1	2	8
5	4000	19000	4200	19600	2	1	3	11
6	4000	23000	4400	24000	1	2	3	14
7	3000	26000	3300	27300	0	0	0	14
8	4000	30000	4200	31500	0	0	0	14
9	4000	34000	3700	35200	2	1	3	17
10 11	3000 3000	37000 40000	5100	40300	1	0	1	18
Appdx	1000	41000†	500	40800				
Proof marks	–	–	= 1500	42300				

* Diagrams not allowed for in word count – but 'textual illustrations' are.

† NOTE: After initially agreeing to a manuscript of 50,000 words in accordance with my synopsis, the publisher asked me to try for 40–45,000 words, in order keep down the cost of production. The word-budget was revised downwards, to reflect the lower limit, after Chapters 1 to 4 had been drafted.

Fig 5.1 The word-budget for this book – targets and achievements in draft.

To understand the significance of the number of words in the book – its length – it is necessary to think about costs and customers' buying characteristics. The cost of type setting, printing and paper is a relatively small proportion of the selling price of the book – see chapter 10. Halving that element of the cost, by producing a shorter book, would not make a great deal of difference to the eventual selling price. If a book scheduled to cost £4.00 were reduced in thickness by half and in cost by as much as 50p, it would almost certainly sell far less well. The book-buying public are often thought to buy books by weight – a thin book appears to offer less value for money. Publishers will try to circumvent this attitude of mind by printing shorter books on thicker paper, but there is a limit to the effectiveness of this approach.

Conversely, an increase in the length of a book, while causing only a small increase in the cost of production, may force the selling price just that little bit too high. A book that appears good value at £4.95 may be psychologically unacceptable at £5.25, even if it does look thicker. Determining the selling price of a new book is a fine balance between production costs and customer resistance. (And who among us today has not thought that a new book looked expensive?)

Organising chapter content

By dividing the subject of our book into more-or-less self-contained chapters and deciding on a word-budget for each chapter we are making the task of writing the book more manageable. We need only think at any one time about writing perhaps five thousand words.

Let us look more closely at the task of writing a single chapter. For the chapter you are now reading, my self-determined word-budget was 4000 words and the original synopsis was:

Writing the book – mechanics: Expanding the synopsis

> into chapter skeletons. Developing within-chapter logic. Work to a word-budget, resulting in agreed number of words. 'Writer is someone who counts words.' – Braine. Importance of a hierarchy of headings. Drafting – longhand, dictate or immediate type. How many drafts? Writing regularly. Links between text and illustrations. Writer's equipment – necessities and niceties.

Most of the ideas are there in the synopsis, but they need expanding. My practice is to take a sheet of lined A4 paper and to write abbreviated synopsis headings spread out down the page. I then expand on the headings, noting down the points that I want to make about each. At the same time I review the logic of the order of the contents. You will see that I decided to start this chapter with the concept of the word-budget rather than with chapter skeletons as in the synopsis. It seemed to me that starting with the word-budget led on more logically from the previous mention of the book length. And it is important to start each chapter with a good lead – something that attracts the reader's attention; that makes him want to continue reading.

Before I start drafting a chapter I put in a lot of work on the sheet with the headings on it – my 'doodles sheet'. Important ideas are written in capitals or ringed to attract attention. Arrows criss-cross the page as the logical order is developed. Sometimes ideas for illustrations develop on this page. Sometimes parts of the chapter are removed to somewhere else in the book; sometimes 'new' parts are brought in from other chapters. The original synopsis is not sacrosanct; in developing the within-chapter logic you are moving into a more detailed level of planning.

Figure 5.2 is a reproduction of the doodling that preceded the writing of this chapter. It shows how my ideas about the order of the contents changed as I thought it through.

The chapter-planning stage should not be ended without deciding some rough idea of the internal word-budget. Just

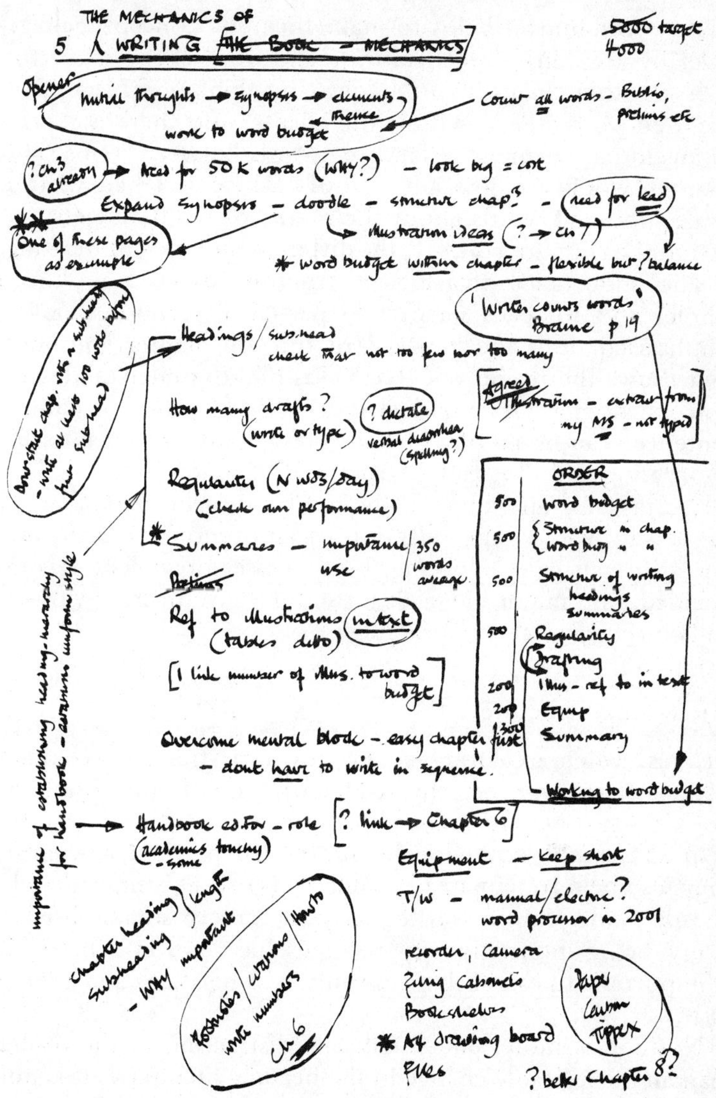

Fig 5.2 A reproduction of the 'doodles sheet' from which I worked in writing this chapter.

as the word-budget helps to make the book concept manageable, by thinking about five-thousand-word chapters; so too does a within-chapter word-budget, by thinking of, say, five-hundred-word items. Within the chapter too there is a need to ensure an adequate balance of words between items. This chapter would be logically out-of-balance if I had written three thousand words about the merits of word-budgets and then only a hundred on, say, the different methods of drafting.

The importance of a logical structure for your book as a whole, and for each chapter in particular, cannot be overemphasised. It is the logical structure of chapter and book that draws the reader on, that helps him to understand what you are saying. Grammatical defects and unclear or clumsy sentences can be rectified by the copy-editor (see chapter 9); re-ordering an illogically structured chapter or book is a major task for an expert in the book's subject. Bad planning can easily lead to the rejection of an otherwise worthwhile book. In our case, adopting the processes previously recommended, any major illogicalities should have been obvious – and corrected – at synopsis stage.

The writing structure

Just as, when exploring a new town, a stranger welcomes signposts, so too does the reader of a non-fiction book. A book's signposts are its headings. Headings within a chapter help the reader to re-locate matters of particular interest; they also help to prepare his thoughts for what is immediately ahead. And, just as traffic signs are largely standardised – many being internationally recognisable – so, in a book, it is important to establish a convention of headings and adhere to it.

Nothing is more amateurish and distracting to the reader than an inexplicable change in the heading hierarchy. It is not common in books, but unfortunately sometimes found in technical journals; one can see a convention of a single stage of bold type, lower case headings at the left of the line, suddenly change to centred headings in capitals, plus italicised lower case subheadings at the left margin. This does nothing more surely than indicate lack of thought.

Before your start to write your book, decide on the hierarchy of headings that you will use throughout. Then stick to it – in every chapter.

The actual typography to be used for the headings is a matter for the publisher's staff to decide – but you must indicate the relative importance of each level of heading. The chapter title is the 'top level' in every hierarchy and can, if necessary, be followed by main section headings, then subheadings, and then by subsidiary or sub-sub-headings should these be necessary. One convention for the typography for such a series of headings is:

A chapter heading – special large, bold, characters;
B main section heading – capitals centred on the line, with space above and below;
C sub-heading – bold characters, perhaps slightly larger than the text, aligned flush with the left margin and with the text commencing on the next line;
D sub-sub-heading – italic characters, otherwise as for sub-heading.

Another convention used by many publishers, including Macmillans, is to refer to chapter headings as 'chapter heading' and the text headings as A, B, C etc in descending order of importance. (The writer should mark the headings in his typescript with the ABCD heading designation. See also chapter 8 for more details on preparing the typescript.)

If the writer has followed the advice already given in this book – to divide his work into self-contained chapter units of 'reasonable' length, it should seldom be necessary to use main section headings (B above). Equally, I have seldom found it necessary to insert sub-sub-headings. In fact, the only occasions when sub-sub-headings have appeared in a book of mine have been when they were added by an over-enthusiastic copy-editor. My strong preference is to use just chapter headings and sub-headings as in this book. And they should then, of course, merely be marked A and B. There is no sacrosanct publishers' convention that side sub-headings are marked 'C'.

Just as, in chapter 3, we suggested that book titles should be brief, so too should both chapter headings and sub-headings. Chapter titles should be kept short because of their use as page headings – *headlines.* Publishers and printers frequently design book layouts to show the book title at the top (or sometimes at the foot) of each left-hand page and the chapter title on each right-hand page. If the titles are more than about 45 characters (counting everything – letters, spaces and punctuation marks) they will not readily fit on the line, which often also has to accommodate the page number. Titles can of course be abbreviated for use in the headlines but this is to be avoided if possible.

Similarly, if sub-headings require almost a full line of space they will not stand out from the page as well as if they were short. The main function of a sub-heading is, as we have said, to act as a signpost for the reader; a subsidiary benefit is the creation of blank space on a page of grey print. Space makes the page look easier to read. A long sub-heading will generate less blank space.

A further consideration in writing sub-headings is their frequent use on the book's contents page. Short sub-headings permit comprehensive chapter content listings without undue waste of space.

There should be neither too many, nor too few, sub-headings. Using fresh sub-headings for every other paragraph is excessive; by interrupting his concentration it will confuse the reader more than it will aid him. Equally, a couple of thousand words between sub-headings leaves the reader short of guidance. My personal preference is for a minimum of about three hundred words and a maximum of about a thousand words to each sub-heading. Inevitably though, any recommendation of this nature is 'more honour'd in the breach than the observance', Clearly there is a close association between the balance of the within-chapter word-budget described at the start of this chapter and the spacing of sub-headings.

In my view, a sub-heading right at the start of a chapter looks wrong. (Some copy-editors will insert headings here, so beware; it has happened to me before now. But see chapter 9 for more about copy-editors.) It is usually possible to avoid this by starting with a general introduction to the chapter's content; this need only be one or two paragraphs in length.

One final personal recommendation related to chapter subdivisions – in technical books I always like to end each chapter with a summary of its contents. A summary can be of immense value to the reader in reviewing the content of each chapter – both immediately after reading and later. The summary should not be too long – it need not be more than 250–300 words – and it can be in the form of notes rather than free-flowing paragraphs.

Drafting

The actual writing of the words to form the book can be accomplished in three ways:

(1) in longhand,
(2) direct on to the typewriter (or a word processor),
(3) by dictating to a machine or to a stenographer.

Many writers today type their thoughts directly on to paper; this can be faster than writing in longhand. Others – blessed with a 'tied' stenographer or audio-typist at home, a complaisant secretary at work, or more money than me – dictate their thoughts for someone else to transcribe. However committed to type, this first effort will inevitably need amending and polishing.

For many years I wrote everything in longhand. That way, I could make changes immediately, as I went along. I could never work direct onto a typewriter; and in any case, I always disliked having to roll back the page to 'paint' out a phrase and replace it. The correcting fluid took too long to dry – and I seldom had a pen to hand while typing. Protagonists of direct typing advocate thinking out a whole sentence before typing it; I find this easier said than done.

Figure 5.3 shows the alterations I made to the first hand-written draft of part of this chapter as I went along.

Today, though, some eight years after this book was written, word processors are everyday office equipment. And word processors are the ideal tool for my 'think-as-you-write' method of writing. When this book was first released, word processors were far too expensive for most writers to afford. Now, thanks to Amstrad, they are within reach of many – from £500 upwards.

A word processor consists of a typewriter-like keyboard, a visual display unit (a screen), a computer, a printer, and a set of electronic instructions to make it all work. (*See* Appendix 3 for more details.) The writer types at the keyboard; his/her words are displayed on the screen. Words, phrases, sentences or whole paragraphs can be corrected, inserted, or removed at will; the order of paragraphs can be re-arranged; and the basic text need only be 'typed' once. When you are satisfied with the words on the screen, the machine will print an immaculate copy. But even then, should you change your mind after printing the 'final' copy, a revised version is available at the touch of a key. You never have to type the whole thing again. There is no such thing as a 'finished' manuscript – until you despatch it.

Back now, though, to before the word processor – and it is perhaps prudent to wait until you can afford one out of your writing earnings. Make sure that your initial drafting is well-spaced. Type in double-spacing; in longhand, write on

8

the timing. And in the third sentence I changed 'I find it inhibiting to need to roll back' to 'I dislike having to roll back', and 'my pen in my hand while typing' to 'my pen at the ready while typing'.

111 B → The whole of the final sentence is a later addition. B (from p9)

56 However committed to paper, the initial draft should be well-spaced. In typing, double-spaced work is essential – with wide margins too. In longhand, write on alternate lines: you will be surprised how often the blank spaces will be used up as you proceed. Fig 5.0 is a reproduction of part of my original first draft.

Once the initial draft of a chapter is complete – whether in longhand or in typescript – it should be reread carefully. Can the ideas be better expressed? Is the order still logical? Is the balance right? Do you want to expand this thought, delete that one or add

49 an afterthought?

C → C from p.9

Counting words

(count individually → later.) While writing, a wise writer checks his output. The novelist, John Braine, in his book Writing a

Fig 5.3 A reproduction of my one and only hand-written draft for part of this chapter. The figures in the left margin are the numbers of words in the adjacent paragraphs.

alternate lines; notice how much of the blank space I used up in Figure 5.3.

Counting words

While writing, a wise writer checks his output. The novelist, John Braine, in his book *Writing a Novel* defines a writer as 'a person who counts words'. The non-fiction writer needs to consider sentence and paragraph lengths (see next chapter); he needs to check on the balance of each chapter's content; and he needs to know how his total output compares with his word-budget. My practice is to count the words individually, by paragraphs – but I am perhaps slightly neurotic about counting words. Many writers, who make fewer amendments than I do, work on an average number of words per line or even per page. I 'count up' every time I have written about five hundred words, or half a dozen paragraphs.

We have already referred to the use of the word-budget as a chapter-by-chapter target. It would be surprising if your writing met the target chapter-lengths exactly; if two or three chapters fall far short of target though, there may well be a need to rethink. Perhaps you are not explaining to the extent that you originally intended or should, or is the word-budget wrong? Can you still produce the necessary number of words in all? Maybe the next chapter or two can be a bit longer, to compensate?

It is worth maintaining a continuous running check on the ups and downs of your output against the word budget.

Figure 5.1, which is the draft word-budget for this book, shows how my chapter-lengths fluctuated from my targets and how I adjusted my writing. I also keep a running check on the number and location of illustrations as I develop these concurrently with the writing. The running word-total of completed chapters may also give you a psychological boost as you sweat over the turn of the next phrase.

It is important not to forget to count ALL the words. Earlier in this chapter we mentioned the need to allow for all parts of the book in developing the word-budget. New writers often forget to count the bibliography, the preface, and sometimes even such things as check-lists. The importance to the publisher of the number of words is directly associated with the cost of producing the book; words in a bibliography cost just as much to print as do 'proper' words in the body of the book.

A writing routine

The actual process of getting words on to paper is made easier by working to a regular routine. Anyone who writes only when the muse moves him is a rank amateur; the professional writes steadily and regularly, on 'good' and 'bad' days alike. It pays to set down – on paper or in your head – a regular target of words per day and per week. As a spare-time writer (and that's a joke – writers never have any spare time) I aim at about four hundred words *every* day plus an *extra* thousand words over the weekend. This is of course only when I am actually in the throes of writing; there are many other activities which precede or follow the writing. My schedule means that I can draft about a chapter a week. This in turn means that, given all the facts I need, I can produce a handwritten book-length draft manuscript in about three months. Redrafting, polishing and typing can then take a further three months.

One of the worst problems for the new writer is actually starting work. Nothing looks more daunting than a blank sheet of paper. A mental block seems to come down at these moments. A few suggestions to help overcome the start-up problem are:

- plan each chapter in advance – see my 'doodles sheet' in figure 5.2.
- start with an easy chapter – or, within a chapter, an easy section. (You do not need to write in sequence; it is often a good idea to write the introductory chapter and any preface last of all, so that they can make reference to what is in store.)
- when you stop writing each day, leave a note for yourself about how you intend to restart – the first few words, the subject, etc.
- if really stuck, read a bit from a competitive book – see how someone else dealt with the subject – a short phrase can often spark off your own line of thought.

Once you have started writing, do not stop for anything. If a sentence will not come right, or if you are short of a fact, leave a gap and fill it in later. Keep the flow of words running while you can. And if the writing is going particularly well one day, carry on as long as possible – do not just stop when you have written the 'required' number of words.

A writer's equipment

Other points about the actual writing of your book fit more readily under the heading of *style*, and are therefore in the next chapter. At this point, however, it may be helpful to look at the physical equipment of a non-fiction author. The days are long gone when a writer could send a handwritten manuscript, in a bundle of child's exercise books, to a publisher with any hope of being considered. For any writer, possession of, or ready access to, a typewriter is essential. Besides this, and paper, most other equipment is usually a nicety rather than a necessity.

Let us then consider equipment necessities and niceties:

- Typewriter – a virtual necessity – can be manual or electric. The advantage of electric typewriters – which are getting cheaper, certainly in real terms – is that they make the work of even an amateur typist look professional.
- Portable tape cassette-recorder – a nicety – can be useful for making notes or recording research interviews. Most now have a built-in microphone, ideal for this purpose.
- Camera – usually a nicety but for some interests can be a necessity. You may wish to record rare material on film for use as book-illustrations; more commonly, ready-made photographs can be obtained from libraries etc. Do not choose a camera with a film size smaller than 35 mm.
- Bookshelves and filing cabinets – almost a necessity, but I suppose the growing number of reference books and papers that you will certainly need can, at least for a time, be stacked on the floor.
- Files – a necessity. You must keep your reference material and your correspondence under systematic control. Your output also needs to be kept safely somewhere. This leads on to a need for a two-hole paper punch and probably a small stapler.
- Drawing board – almost a necessity for the technical writer, who will at least have to prepare good rough sketches for the publisher's artist (see chapter 7). Very suitable A4 boards are available at a relatively small cost, complete with substitute-tee-square; I have used one such board for several years.

Summary

(1) Before starting to write, decide on a word-budget for your book. This should provisionally allocate numbers of words to each chapter as targets to ensure the agreed overall book-length. Big differences in book-length from that agreed with the publisher can affect its commercial potential.

(2) For each chapter, expand the original synopsis into a chapter skeleton – a page of doodles – as you build up the content and sequence. Within the chapter skeleton, decide on a rough word-budget for different sections, to ensure a balanced chapter content.

(3) Decide on a standard system of within-chapter headings – they will form the reader's essential signposts. One 'level' of headings below the chapter title is usually enough, but for some technical books there can be main section headings, sub-headings, and sub-sub-headings, all within each chapter.

(4) Sub-headings – like chapter titles – need to be brief, perhaps four or five words at most, to ensure their effectiveness. Sub-headings should be well-spaced. There should seldom be two sub-headings on a single page of print, nor should sub-headings often be more than the turn of the page apart.

(5) Books can be written, initially, in longhand, or directly on to the typewriter, or they can be dictated. Longhand drafting permits polishing of the text as it is written, but it is usually slower than direct-to-type drafting. Dictation has been known to induce verbal diarrhoea.

(6) Writers should count their words virtually as they write them; if you are unwilling to become too obsessed, the average number of words per line and per page can be used as a quick measure.

(7) Regular writing, to a specific target of completed words, is a necessary part of the professional approach. The

muse is not an adequate prod to persuade you to tackle the vast expanse of a blank page; a writer needs to be disciplined.

(8) The only absolutely essential piece of equipment for a writer is a typewriter – or at least access to one. Book manuscripts MUST be typed. (see chapter 8.)

6
The writing itself

I notice that you use plain, simple language, short words and brief sentences. That is the way to write English. It is the modern way and the best way. Stick to it.

Mark Twain

This book is not written for the potential literary genius; he needs no help from me. You, the reader, are an ordinary person, capable of writing, but perhaps not as fluently as you would wish. The easy way of advising you on writing-style is to say that the way to learn to write well, is to practise. Write down your thoughts and ideas; read them back to yourself and then rewrite them – better. Write, polish and rewrite. But this advice is facile and less than helpful.

There is no doubt that good writing is hard work. Sheridan got it right when he said, 'You write with ease, to show your breeding, but easy writing's curst hard reading.' To write well requires a lot of thought, a lot of consideration of, and for, the target reader. We met Abdul Helena McChang in chapter 3. As you write, think back repeatedly, 'Will AHMcC understand what I have just written?'

Writing-style can be improved by exposure to good writing. A good writer is a writer who reads, and a non-fiction writer should extend his reading beyond other non-fiction books, to read good fiction too. But the non-fiction author needs to be wary of the colourful descriptive passages sometimes included in novels. These are seldom appropriate in a non-fiction book. Remember always, the aim of a non-fiction book is to convey the writer's knowledge to the reader. So long as the message is communicated, the literary quality of the prose is of limited importance, and may even get in the way.

So long as the non-fiction writer expresses himself correctly, logically and clearly, any minor defects in writing style can – and will – be rectified by the copy-editor (see chapter 9). Throughout one of my books I consistently misspelt the word accommodate (using only one m); luckily the copy-editor corrected this for me. Editors have also, on occasions, corrected my careless split infinitives. So, do not worry too much – but try hard to get it right yourself. If you get it right first time the style will remain yours, not the copy-editor's.

Basic guidelines

While writing-style is a matter of personal choice, there are a few guidelines – not 'rules' – that will help. Break them intentionally if you will, but not by accident. In summary the basic guidelines are:

- always think of and write for the target reader (AHMcC);
- let your writing be accurate;
- let your writing be brief – concise rather than short;
- let your writing be clear and simple – again, think of AHMcC.

And the final three guidelines can be considered as the ABC of writing – let it be A accurate, B brief, C clear.

At the well-justified risk of continued repetition – for it is perhaps the most important concept of all in non-fiction writing – aim at the target reader. Your purpose is to reach the reader; if you do not, you are crying in the wilderness. And it must NEVER appear as though you are *writing down* to the reader. Nothing will more dissuade him from buying or reading your book than a patronising attitude. Think of the reader as equally as intelligent a person as yourself – merely less aware of your particular subject. A farmer from the Australian outback reading one of my transportation books might conceivably be starting from 'square one' – but were I reading a book he had written on sheep farming, I would myself be similarly unaware. Knowledge depends on where you are standing; writing a book about something does not, of itself, merit a universal superior status. Humility is a necessary characteristic of a non-fiction writer.

The need for your writing to be accurate is obvious – but merits restating. Readers will refer to your book, treating its contents as fact – unless they are obviously and clearly differentiated as opinions. One silly mistake can damn an otherwise authoritative book. The research process described in chapter 2 should ensure that the facts you write are correct. But accuracy has other aspects.

One major task for the writer is to check back on what he has written, to ensure that it is still exactly what he intended. It is too easy to change the meaning of a sentence by a subsequently inserted clause. Words too, the meaning of which you are sure you know, should be checked in the dictionary – not just for meaning, but also for spelling. Time and again I find my convictions about the meaning and spelling of a supposedly well-known word are unfounded. I check my words frequently, trying to avoid using them loosely. Every writer's dictionary should be well-thumbed.

The recommendations for brevity and simple clarity in non-fiction writing will, of themselves, do much to generate a 'good' style. And in this sense, 'good' means no more than effective; concise, clear writing will ease the reader's progress to understanding.

Brevity

While overall shortness is a decided virtue in, for example, management or technical writing, when writing a non-fiction book there is more room to expand. But this does not mean that there is room for unnecessary waffle or padding. Writing should be taut – free from superfluous words – yet expansive where detail is necessary. Few are the authors whose work could not be improved by a judicious trimming of unnecessary words. And I do not exclude myself from that criticism; could I not have done better without the 'decided' in the first line of this paragraph?

The cost of typesetting 'too many' words can have a significant effect on the cost of a book with a small initial print run. Typesetting and similar work, such as artwork, can account for as much as a third of the cost of production (typesetting, paper, printing and binding). See chapter 10 for more details on how a book price is made up.

Of greater effect on writing-style, the brevity recommendation should also be applied to words, sentences and paragraphs:

- always use a short word in preference to a long word – even if this means that you need two or three short words to replace a single longer one. Short words are more easily understood than longer ones.
- try to keep sentences as short as possible. I try to work to an average sentence length of 16 words and a maximum of 25 words. But in that latter respect I sometimes fail. The basic rule should be to restrict all sentences to a single statement. I would not criticise the long sentence just for being long; but to write a long sentence well and clearly requires great care. Short sentences are easier to write. They are certainly easier to understand (see figure 6.1). Short sentences have the added advantage of being simpler to punctuate; commas and full-stops will usually suffice.

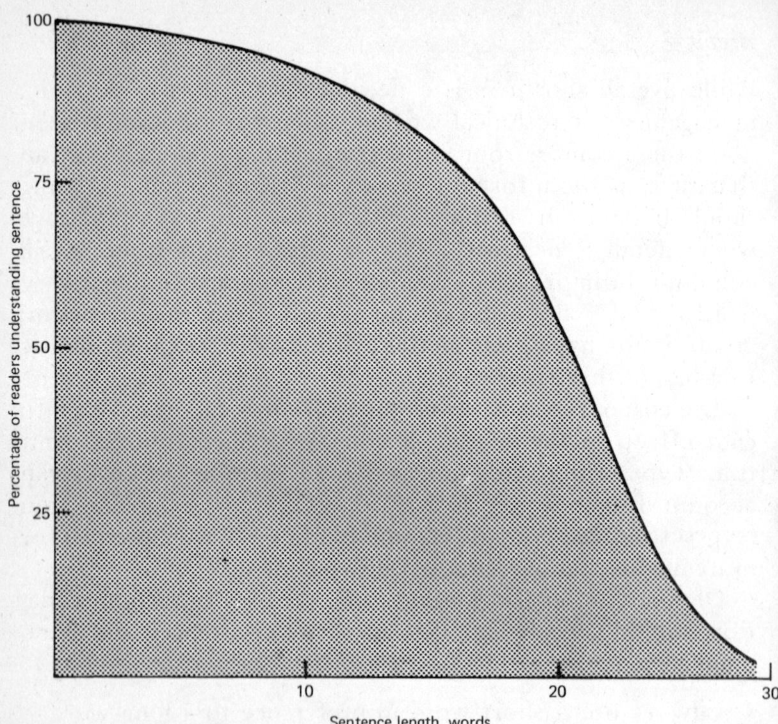

Fig 6.1 The significance of the sentence length in the average reader's understanding – based on an American survey.

- paragraphs should be restricted to a single thought. This thought may often be expressed in the first sentence and elaborated on in subsequent sentences. I like to restrict the length of my paragraphs to a maximum of about 160 words and an average of under 80. In my initial drafting I frequently find that I have inadvertently written a paragraph containing as many as two hundred words. Reviewing the content of these long paragraphs, I can almost always split them into two and sometimes even three shorter – and better – paragraphs.

Although the previous paragraph mentions specific sentence and paragraph lengths, these recommendations should not be applied too rigidly. If I were to write entirely in the shortest sentences, my writing would appear jerky and abrupt. Similarly, a uniform set of eighty-word paragraphs would make an extremely dull-looking page. For an effective writing-style, vary the sentence and paragraph lengths. But strive to work within the maximum lengths recommended above. Observe how I intersperse short sentences and short paragraphs among longer ones – and vice versa.

The advice in this section reinforces that in the previous chapter about counting words. Unless you count the words that you write, it is too easy to become long-winded. A long-winded writer is a poor writer. Count your words to improve your style.

Clarity

Every writer should try at all times to write clearly. It is only the inadequate, the incompetent, or the pompous writer who feels a need to wrap up his thoughts in gobbledegook. It is never right to seek to impress the reader with the extent of your knowledge or your ability, nor to show how profound is your thinking. As a writer, your object is to communicate – to convey your message to your reader. It is for this reason that it is so important to visualise Abdul Helena McChang, your target reader, as accurately as possible.

The best way of writing clearly is to write simply. Think of English as one language – not as a spoken language and a different written language – and *write like you talk.* (And here I acknowledge my debt to Robert Gunning's book *The Technique of Clear Writing*, for the idea of the ungrammatical 'write like' rather than the correct, but less clear, 'write as'.) Figure 6.2 suggests a few words and phrases that are best avoided in your writing – but there are many many more such.

- *and* (in the middle of a long sentence) – in such a position, it can probably be replaced by a full-stop, thereby improving the writing.

- *jargon* – jargon is permissible when writing exclusively for those who understand it. The author of a non-fiction book is 'teaching' those who would not understand jargon. He should not normally use it, but a jargon expression may sometimes be worth explaining for the reader's future reference.

- *buzz-words* – nothing grates on the reader more than the use of coined words, such as *company-wise, policy-wise, hospitalise.* Avoid them.

- *I are/is* – in this form, not a common error, but when subject and verb are widely separated in a sentence, with interposing subsidiary clauses, it is not difficult to get the tense wrong. Avoid the problem by keeping sentences short – and checking subject/verb compatibility.

- *padding* – the written equivalents of the spoken *ums* and *ers.* Examples of such woolly pauses for thought include:
  'It should be noted (or emphasised) that . . . '
  'As indicated . . . '
  'In fact . . . '
  'Clearly . . . '

- *the impersonal* – why avoid saying 'I did this – or that . . . '? If it was you, say so. Anonymity is not an automatic virtue.

- *in the case of* – seldom necessary, for example, 'In the case of Blank's batteries, their duration of output is greater.' (Greater than what?) This could be better expressed as, 'Blank's batteries last longer.'

Fig 6.2 Words and phrases to be avoided whenever possible.

As you write, think to yourself, 'Would I say that? Or would a listener make it clear by his expression that I was sounding pompous, wordy and unclear?' A speaker has the advantage of instant visual feedback from his listeners and can adjust the level of his talk to ensure that they understand. The writer has no such feedback. Again, this explains the need for the clear characterisation of the target reader. A writer should write at such a level that comprehension – by AHMcC – is assured: but without 'writing down'. You are striving for a smooth, non-flowery, flow of words and thoughts. I find it helpful to say my words to myself as I write them. And as an example of this, look back at the end of the second sentence in this paragraph. I first wrote '. . . to ensure comprehension', but when I read it through that sounded a bit pompous. I amended it to what I might have *said*, '. . . to ensure that they understand'. I think that this is an improvement.

You must be careful in *writing like you talk*. Many people speak English loosely, without finishing sentences and with expressive pauses. Some people speak badly. What I am advising is that you write as you wish you spoke – simply and expressively, using familiar words, but without excessive colloquialism.

The act of *writing like you talk* will almost certainly ensure that you meet the next recommendation – that you use simple, familiar words. And again, the advice in the section on brevity, to use short words in preference to long ones, even if this means using more words, will lead to the use of simple words.

Punctuation too, can and should be kept simple. Again, this recommendation goes hand-in-hand with the advice to keep sentences short. The purpose of punctuation is to help to make the writing clear. Punctuate therefore, only as much as is necessary to make the meaning clear. It is only the longer sentences that need a lot of punctuation; short sentences are well served by commas and full-stops alone. A comma

,	comma – a pause. The second most useful punctuation point. Separates clauses in a sentence.
;	semi-colon – a longer pause. Used to separate thoughts not quite complete in themselves. Use sparingly and with great care.
:	colon – almost a full-stop. Used to link separate and complete thoughts in a longer sentence, for instance, where the second thought arises naturally from the first. Also used alone, without a dash, to introduce a list. Use with care.
.	full-stop or period – the end of a sentence complete in itself. The most useful punctuation point of all. USE IT FREQUENTLY.
!	exclamation mark – self-explanatory. Should be used sparingly – excessive use of 'the screamer' is the mark of an amateur writer.
"	quote marks (quotes) – note the normal use of single quotes for all purposes. Double quote marks should be used for quotations within the main quote.

Fig 6.3 Punctuation – an incomplete introduction to the most useful points.

indicates a pause, a full-stop the end of a statement. A colon is almost a full-stop: it is a means whereby two short sentences may well be joined. It is also the correct introduction to a list of related items; it does not need the addition of a dash. Figure 6.3 elaborates on the more useful punctuation points.

The final recommendation to assist you in writing clearly is to use active verbs rather than passive ones. Thus, the statement,

> This book was written by Gordon Wells,

which is passive, would be clearer and therefore better, in the active form,

Gordon Wells wrote this book.

A common use of the passive form in management writing is the phrase,

It is recommended that . . .

but who recommended it? It is far better, if less safe for the writer, to say,

I (or we) recommend that . . .

The content of the writing

Moving on from matters of the writer's style, let us look at what you will write, and how to get started. There are four useful pieces of advice for the beginner:

- start the book, and each chapter, with a bang. Try to think up a good 'lead' – something that will entice the reader to start reading.
- within sections of a chapter it is often a good idea to list several aspects of the section's subject and then go on to expand on each in turn. I have used this technique several times in this book. This layout of the text is an acceptable technique in a technical non-fiction book; it would not be so acceptable in, for example, a history book, where the listing might be better contained in a long, flowing, paragraph.
- wherever possible, appeal to the reader's self-interest. You are writing expressly for Abdul Helena McChang: say, 'you should do this'. (Better still, say 'If you do this, this will happen.') Extend this where possible by linking your advice to the target reader's likely experience.
- wherever possible, intersperse your writing with relevant examples or anecdotes – how you or someone else dealt with the problem you are discussing. Always make your descriptions understandable to the reader – for example, it may be better to say that a lamp-standard is as high as a two-storey house than to say it is so many metres high.

Many non-fiction books, and particularly technical ones, are improved by the inclusion of illustrations and tables. Think about appropriate illustrations while writing the associated text, not later as an afterthought. It is unfortunately not uncommon to find illustrations seemingly quite unrelated to the words that surround them. And you should refer to the illustration in the text. The reference need be no more than a mere 'See figure 0.0', or it can be something like, 'figure 0.0 is a flow-chart of the process we are about to describe.' It is unwise to say 'figure 0.0 *above*' for the printer may not be able to fit the illustration in above the reference – it may be below. The choice and preparation of illustrations is discussed in chapter 7 and their place in the final manuscript in chapter 8.

Tables are a particularly effective way of providing the reader of a technical non-fiction book with detailed, often numerical, information. They should however be used as sparingly as possible; a page of tabular material may cost as much to typeset as several pages of ordinary text. Make all of your tables worth their cost; include a table only where it is absolutely necessary.

The best tables are simple and easy to read. The bigger and more complex a table becomes, the more difficult to understand and expensive to set it becomes. And at all times strive to restrict table widths to what can be accommodated across the *upright* page. You will not always achieve this goal but an upright table is far easier to take in than one for which the reader has to turn the page round.

Treat tables as illustrations; do not include them in the text unless they are extremely small – two or three lines only. The printer will fit the table in as near to your textual reference as possible, but he cannot readily guarantee to complete it on a given page if it is not separated from the text. And nothing looks worse than an unheaded bottom-half of a table at the top of a new page. Depending on your publisher's house style, give each table a number – 'Table 0.0', or conceivably 'Figure 0.0' – and where appropriate, a title. The title should clearly indicate the content of the table and, where appropriate, should contain details of the source of the data.

Still favoured by some academic writers, footnotes should, as far as possible, be avoided by any writer striving to be professional. Footnotes are not liked by publishers because they push up the costs of typesetting. Too often, footnotes are either the afterthoughts of an amateurish writer, a private discussion between rival professors, or material which rightly belongs in the body of the text. They are always a distraction to the reader and a nuisance to the printer – particularly if they run on over more than one page.

None of the previous paragraph is meant to deny the citing of references in the text. These can effectively be handled by consecutive *superior* (raised above the line and usually small) numbers in the text and corresponding sources or notes at the end of each chapter or of the whole book.

A final point about writing content – how to write numbers. Few of us would think of writing 'There are 2 alternatives . . . '; we would usually write, without thinking, 'There are two alternatives . . . '. Similarly, it would be unusual to write, 'The park had space for one-hundred-and-sixty-nine cars.' Our automatic reaction is to write, 'The park had space for 169 cars.' But where do we change from spelling out numbers in full to using numerals? It is conventional to spell out numbers up to ten and to use figures thereafter. Another easily remembered convention is to spell out all single-word numbers, that is one to twenty; and to use numerals for 21 (twenty-one) and above. If you were saying 'Fifty-odd people came to the party,' the number would be spelt out because it is not meant to be precise; 51 people would be set in numerals, as would 50 per cent. (And avoid starting a sentence with a numeral. Instead say, 'The party was attended by 51 people.') In lists of numbers it is best to stick to one form even if this does mean breaking some of the above conventions. And remember always to use numerals in conjunction with any form of unit.

After writing – check

I have already stressed the importance of re-reading what you have written to ensure that it still says what you meant. It is also worth repeating – once again – the benefits of checking sentence and paragraph lengths, and of checking that your words are as simple as possible.

Read through your work yet again. Check whether that extra long paragraph really is all one *thought*: if not, it is almost certainly better split into two. Consider again whether the meaning of that long sentence will be clear to your target reader. A long sentence can almost always be simplified by making it into two or more shorter ones.

Look carefully at all the long words that have slipped in. Remember: a long word is usually *hard* to understand. (But differentiate between *easy* words made long by prefixes and suffixes, which are still easy, and long words that are *hard* 'in their own right'.) If too many long hard words have slipped into your writing, the whole text will be *hard.* So rewrite them out: substitute easier, shorter, words. Remember: your aim is to communicate with your reader – not to impress him with your *erudition.* (And that is a good example of a long word that I should rewrite out. I should have said – not to show him how clever you are.)

And – check your spelling.

Editing others' contributions

We have already referred to the possibility of compiling a book, the chapters of which are contributed by individual experts. A book like this is often known as a handbook. It needs an editor; you may be selected by the publisher as knowing the field well enough to bring the right people together. Or you may 'sell' the idea to the publisher. Either way, you will be required to edit your colleagues' contributions. And there's the rub.

It requires considerable skill, both professional or technical and literary, to edit a compilation of others' work. It also requires tact. The tasks that have to be undertaken include:

- establishing a degree of continuity throughout the book. This necessitates the prior allocation and careful review of chapter content at synopsis stage, and again when written. Beware not only of overlapping chapter contents, but also particularly of disagreements over fact or principle. (It is surprising how many 'facts' are subject to differences of 'interpretation'.)
- establishing an appearance of uniformity throughout the book. This necessitates at least the establishment (and enforcement) of a common system of headings and subheadings. It may also involve establishing a common approach to illustrations, tables, etc.
- checking contributions for 'readability'. I would probably first check paragraph lengths – by checking numbers of lines of typescript – and later by delving into the longer paragraphs. Obviously the editor must read all the contributions. As I read them I would lightly mark all long words – perhaps at first only those that I did not myself find familiar. There is then the tactical problem of persuading a colleague that his writing is unnecessarily hard to understand. You, the editor, will usually need to rewrite phrases, retaining the meaning while simplifying the language, and obtain the contributor's permission for the changes. It is essential that you edit out all 'academic gobbledegook'.
- checking word choice, spelling and punctuation. There will be many faults.
- last but not least, ensuring that the publisher's timetable is adhered to. This is an almost impossible task – it is certainly thankless.

Summary

(1) Good writing is hard work. It should be plain and simple. It will be improved if the writer reads the works of others – fiction as well as non-fiction.

(2) Good writing is basically a product of good manners – think first, last, and all the time of the reader.

(3) Make your writing accurate – in respect of factual content, of word-meaning, and of spelling. Nothing more damns a book than minor errors; they make the reader wonder where the big ones are.

(4) Let your writing be concise, shorn of padding, free from verbiage, yet complete in its explanations of aspects new to the reader. Let the words, sentences and paragraphs be as short as possible, consistent with clarity and variety.

(5) Let your writing be simple, and therefore clear to the reader. Think always whether or not you would say what you are writing – or whether the listener would greet you with a glazed look of incomprehension. Let your punctuation also be simple.

(6) Search for an attention-grabbing opening to each new chapter; drag the reader in by the scruff of his neck. Then hold him, by working on his particular self-interests.

(7) Separate illustrations and tables from the main run of the text and refer to them in the text. The printer will put them as close as possible to the right place but they cannot be positioned exactly.

(8) After writing, check your work for its readability. Can you read it aloud with *ease*?

(9) A handbook editor needs to ensure continuity and conformity between chapters, a uniform appearance, and an appropriate readability – free from gobbledegook.

7
Illustrating the book

'What is the use of a book,' thought Alice, 'without pictures . . . ?' And there is a lot to be said for Alice's view. Every non-fiction book is improved by good illustrations. But today, illustrations have to be worth their cost and their space. They have to earn their place.

What then are the functions of an illustration in a non-fiction book? They are, in random order:

- to help the reader to visualise something more easily than he could by reading a description or trying to absorb columns of figures; to make the description 'come alive'.
- to picture a process where, for instance, it would be difficult to describe the concurrence of several activities as well as they could be drawn – for example in a flow-chart.
- to break up the text – to relieve the areas of grey print.
- to improve the attractiveness of the book's appearance – to make it look good, to help it to sell.

Illustrations are important. They are the first things that most people notice as they idly flip the pages of a book in a shop or library. An American tabloid newspaper magnate is reported to have said that a good picture was worth a thousand words of print. In today's world of increasing book production costs, however, it is essential to be sure that the illustrations in your book are worth that thousand words. Illustrations can cost more than the text-space that they occupy.

An illustration should be a complement to the text. It should enhance the text rather than duplicate an already adequate description. It should of itself be informative, if only in clarifying the text. It should of course be pertinent to the main theme of the text and not to a side-issue. The selection or the design of illustrations for a non-fiction book is therefore very much a process of excluding the interesting or picturesque in favour of the essential. Your aim should be quality rather than quantity.

Types of illustration

To the writer and the reader the illustrations in a book can be categorised as being either pictorial or diagrammatic. This classification is based solely on appearance. (Words in 'boxes', such as figure 1.1 in this book, are sometimes treated as illustrations for the purpose of numbering figures, but this is of course merely a convention.) To the printer, however, illustrations are either *half-tone* or *line*. This classification is based not on appearance but on the tonal content of the illustration itself. And although most half-tone illustrations are pictorial and most diagrammatic illustrations are line drawings, there is no inevitable link between the writer/reader illustration classification and that of the printer.

Most half-tone illustrations will be photographs. Any illustration, however, that includes an area of continuous tone – which can vary in depth – has to be treated as a half-tone illustration. The tone can be a painted wash, a photographic image or pencil shading; anything that produces a continuous block of tone. It is solely this continuous area of tone that differentiates half-tone illustrations from line drawings, which can offer very similar effects by the use of closely-spaced black dots.

Line illustrations are what the name implies – pictures built up of lines, plus dots and/or solid black areas. Every line, dot or solid black area will be printed equally black; the appearance of tone is created by the spacing and size of the lines or dots.

The printer's differentiation between line and half-tone illustrations derives from the different methods used in the past for printing them. Line illustrations could be made into metal blocks for setting alongside, and printing simultaneously with, the text matter. Half-tone illustrations were made into blocks that had to be printed on glossy 'art paper' – as *plates.* Half-tone blocks cost considerably more than line blocks.

This differentiation is still appropriate today for books produced by letterpress. (In the letterpress process lines of type are cast in hot metal, the resultant *slug*, or line of type, having raised reversed letters on it, rather like typewritter keys.) Usually it is only those non-fiction books with smaller print-runs that are now produced by letterpress. For these, line illustrations are still much preferred. Half-tone illustrations in the inevitable separate Plate section will be expensive. They are probably not worth their cost in a technical non-fiction book. They may of course, be essential in, say, a historical or travel book; the overall approach to the illustrations should then be discussed with the publisher as early as possible. It may be that the book can be produced differently – to make the inclusion of half-tone illustrations less costly and thus more acceptable.

Increasingly, non-fiction books with a largish print-run are being produced by lithography. Lithography does not necessitate the use of individually formed metal print characters or the preparation of metal blocks for illustrations. It enables a wide variety of tones to be printed without the need for art paper. Illustrations need to be properly prepared for litho-printing but cast metal blocks are not required and the cost of using line or half-tone illustrations is about the same.

The use of lithographic printing methods therefore permits

the use, throughout the text, of either half-tone or line illustrations as appropriate.

Unless agreed in advance by the publisher – and this is unlikely – do not even think about colour illustrations for your non-fiction book. Colour is very expensive; it is seldom if ever justified in other than mass-market, 'coffee-table' type, non-fiction books.

Another type of illustration to avoid is the over-large one. Occasionally – usually in older books – one sees a large folded illustration, usually a map, set in a book. These oversize illustrations have to be printed separately from the book, carefully folded, and individually inserted in ('tipped in') the book; this is now prohibitively expensive and must always be avoided.

Line illustrations

Most line illustrations in non-fiction books will be diagrams. That is, they will not necessarily purport to portray a subject as viewed; their purpose is rather to show clearly all relevant features.

A drawing prepared for any other purpose is unlikely to be a good line illustration for a book. Book illustrations should be prepared specifically for the purpose. They should be:

- simple and uncluttered – too much detail can confuse the reader;
- well-labelled – but not excessively, for the same reason as above (a limit of 25 words of labelling is a good target);
- clear – there should be no doubt about the illustration's purpose;
- large enough to use most of the available space to the full (see below).

In seeking to meet the above requirements it is helpful to consider the size of the illustrations in a book. Increasingly, many non-fiction books are produced in what is known as *metric Demy octavo* size – a page-size of 216 x 138 mm. Of greater importance is the type area of the book, for illustrations seldom extend beyond the boundaries of the type. For a metric Demy octavo book the dimensions of the *usual* type area are 100 mm width and 170 mm depth; within this must be allowed 5 mm depth for each line of caption.

The other common size for technical books is *metric Royal octavo* with a page size of 234 x 156 mm and a type area of 110 x 190 mm.

Illustrations can be either upright ('portrait') or horizontal ('landscape'). It is always an inconvenient distraction for a reader to have to rotate the book to study a 'landscape' illustration that fills a page. Wherever possible therefore avoid large horizontal diagrams that need the full type area. Smaller horizontal diagrams that can be accommodated within the 100 mm 'un-rotated' width are of course acceptable. Tall, thin, diagrams too should be avoided wherever possible; anything that occupies less than about two-thirds of the type width will look odd. Some illustrations will consist of several parts which can be laid out to occupy the full extent of the space. (Figure 9.2 later in this book is a particularly relevant example of this approach.) Often too, two smaller individual illustrations to which reference is made within perhaps about a thousand words of text, can be brought together to fill the type area. (The thousand-word criterion is intended to ensure that words and relevant text would together extend over not more than the turn of a page, the illustrations being placed roughly half-way through the related text.)

Many of the line illustrations that I use myself – like some in this book – are variations on flow-charts, describing processes. Diagrams of this type can almost always be so laid out as to ensure that they are upright and fill the type width; it is merely a question of scale.

Diagrammatic illustrations need not necessarily be restricted to representations of an artefact or to flow-charts. Other types of diagram that should be carefully considered in designing illustrations include:

- graphs – these can be of two types: conceptual, where the shape is more important than the scale; and detailed, where scale is important to convey numerical information. (Figures 6.1 and 10.1 are particularly appropriate uses of graphical illustrations.)
- bar charts – useful for displaying and comparing quantities over time or by area, such as 'production of widgets in 1905, 1915 and 1925', or 'numbers of widgeters operating in Australia, the Americas, Africa, and Europe'.
- pie charts – particularly useful for displaying the parts of a whole. (To convert percentages to degrees, for setting out a pie chart, multiply by 3.6.)

Who draws – and how?

Who is to prepare the line illustrations for a book is something that needs to be agreed with the publisher. Some publishers will wish to have the drawings prepared by their own staff, working from sketches (*roughs*) prepared by the author. Others may look to you to prepare suitable drawings – usually with the exception of the lettering. But this is often something that can be negotiated. If you are a lousy artist, the publisher will not want to spoil the book for a ha'porth of artwork. But if a lot of artwork is involved, your inability to help may tip the balance of the book's commercial acceptability.

The rough sketches from which the publisher will produce finished artwork should not be too rough. The roughs are all that the publisher's draughtsman has to work from; he will not read your manuscript. The draughtsman can only produce more polished, more typographically appropriate, more sophisticated, versions of your originals. Often he will trace directly from the roughs, merely adjusting the 'weight' of the lines for better appearance.

Whether you have agreed to prepare finished but unlettered artwork or just roughs, you need to consider the drawing size. Most line illustrations are printed smaller than the originals – to hide minor blemishes – which is the same as saying that they should be drawn larger than the final intended size. It is particularly important that all drawings, finished or rough, are prepared for the same degree of reduction. This is because whole batches of drawings are usually reduced together, in a single process. The most commonly adopted reduction factors are 50 per cent and 67 per cent – that is originals are drawn twice and one-and-a-half times print size. This means that, with a 50 per cent reduction factor and a 100 mm x 170 mm type area, the actual drawings should be made between about 140 mm (two-thirds of the width) and 200 mm wide, and up to 330 mm deep (allowing for a one-line caption).

Because it is to be reduced in size, not only does the original drawing need to be 'larger than life', but so too do the lines with which it is drawn. For most drawings, two or three different line thicknesses (*weights*) should suffice. At print size, these are:

lightest	0.1–0.15 mm
normal	0.3 mm
heaviest	0.4 mm

At a 50 per cent reduction factor, these line widths will be 0.25, 0.6 and 0.8 mm and at 67 per cent reduction factor, 0.2, 0.4 and 0.6 mm. You would be wise to use a proper draughtsman's pen, such as that marketed by Rotring. I have successfully prepared many of the illustrations in my technical books, however, with an ordinary, but new, fibre-tip pen, but this requires great care, to ensure constant line thickness. Another essential is a good strong black ink of consistent density – hence my emphasis on a *new* fibre-tip pen.

Final artwork should either be done on good quality

tracing paper or on cartridge paper – but, again, publishers have always accepted my drawings on thick typing paper. My own practice is to prepare both roughs and finished artwork on A4 paper, using a Rotring 'Rapid' A4 drawing board, complete with built-in set-square. There are, of course, other makes of A4 drawing board available, but I have always found the Rotring one ideal. The advantages of working exclusively on A4-sized paper are twofold: there is no problem with despatching oversize material to the publisher, everything is on A4 paper; and the dimensions of an A4 sheet 297 mm x 210 mm conveniently accommodate a virtually full-page illustration at both 50 per cent and 67 per cent reduction factors.

When preparing roughs I indicate all the lettering in ink directly on to the original – in capital letters to avoid misinterpretation. When preparing finished artwork, I make a photocopy of the drawing without lettering. I then letter up the copy – which is itself copied for my retention – and send original and lettered-up copy to the publisher.

Half-tone illustrations

Most half-tone illustrations in non-fiction books are photographs. A very small number may perhaps be early coloured prints or pencil drawings, but even these are probably better photographed – professionally. Photographs for use as book illustrations need to be:

- black and white – that is, not colour-prints and preferably not even black and white prints from colour negatives.
- sharp – that is, well-focused.
- printed on glossy rather than matt paper.
- well-contrasted – without being 'soot and whitewash'.
- larger than print size – 200 mm x 150 mm is a good minimum standard size. Like line illustrations, photo-

graphs are usually reproduced at a considerable reduction factor.

- full of the subject – let the subject of the photograph fill the picture. Avoid the sort of photograph where 'Auntie Lucy is that headless person over in the top left corner'.
- unmounted – but if already mounted, do not court damage by trying to separate.

It is not necesary for the author of a non-fiction book to take all the photographs himself. It is often better not to do so, unless he is an expert photographer. Many photographs suitable for use in technical non-fiction books can be obtained from the public relations offices of firms, trade organisations or government departments, from photographic agencies, or from libraries, museums and the like. Prints from commercial organisations and government departments can sometimes be obtained free of charge, other sources will of course require payment. It is also essential to obtain permission in writing for the use of the pictures in your book. This will usually be subject to acknowledgement of the source, either in the caption or on an acknowledgements page. In the final resort it may be necessary to commission a professional photographer to take pictures that would otherwise be unobtainable.

Preparing illustrations for delivery

All illustrations, whether line or half-tone, should be numbered. If half-tone illustrations are to be included in a letterpress production they should be separately numbered, as Plate 1, Plate 2, etc. The number of plates will have been agreed with the publisher: do not forget, however, that there can be two or more smaller half-tone pictures on a single plate. Number them Plate 1A, 1B, etc.

If the book is to be produced by lithography, all illustrations, line and half-tone, should be numbered consecutively by chapter, thus: Fig 1.1, Fig 1.2 . . . ; Fig 2.1; Fig 3.1, Fig

3.2. If line illustrations only are to be used in a letterpress book, follow the same numbering convention.

With line illustrations, mark the figure number, your name, and the reduction factor on the face of the drawing – but outside the used, or print, area. On photographs, mark your name and the figure (or plate) number *very lightly*, in ink (NOT ball-pen or pencil) on the *reverse* of the print. Beware of pressing too hard or using too sharp a writing implement; this can cause a flaw in the surface which will show up in the book itself.

Should it ever be necessary to indicate required artwork on a photograph – for example, an area to be masked out, or an arrow or reference number to be inserted – fold a sheet of thin paper over the print, fasten it on the back with adhesive tape, and mark the requirements on the overlay. Be careful to use only the softest of pencils, and that very lightly, for marking on the overlay, for fear of indenting the print itself. The overlay can be unfolded and the masks and lines over-drawn in ink if necessary.

Finished drawings, roughs and photographs should be grouped together, separately from the typescript, and sorted into order, before delivery to the publisher. On no account should any illustration be stuck on to the pages of type-script (nor, even worse, draw there); the illustrations are not processed by the people who handle the text. If photographs do not have their own overlays, it is sensible to interleave them with sheets of thin typing paper. My preference is to put all illustrations into a separate envelope, together with a brief list of the contents. Captions would not normally be included with the illustrations – captions have to be typeset in common with the rest of the text – but an additional photocopy of the caption sheets (see below) makes an excel-lent check list.

Captions

We have already mentioned that the illustrations are one of

the first, and therefore most important, things that a reader looks at in a book. And when he looks at the illustration he reads the caption. The captions are probably the most-read parts of the whole book. It is important therefore to get them right. They should state clearly what the illustration is and, where appropriate, the source of the information on which it is based. Captions are not the place to insert those extra items of information that you forgot to include in the text, yet the caption should be complete in itself. In some instances, captions could well meet the newspaper criterion of specifying, the five Ws and an H: Who? What? Why? Where? When? and How? But these questions are less appropriate in the conventional technical non-fiction book.

Captions should be typed in list format, numbered to correspond with the illustrations. Like all other parts of the typescript (see next chapter), the captions should be typed in double spacing on A4 paper. Several copies of the caption list will be useful.

Summary

(1) An illustration can be worth a thousand words of text. It is up to the writer to ensure that each illustration *is* worth that much; illustrations can cost more than text.

(2) Illustrations should complement the text, explaining something that is not, and cannot be, otherwise included in the text. Before including an illustration, consider whether or not it is essential, or just interesting.

(3) For short print-run technical non-fiction books, printed by letterpress, illustrations may be limited to line drawings. If, in this case, a few half-tone illustrations were absolutely essential – and worth the considerable extra cost – they would be printed as plates on glossy art paper.

(4) For books with bigger print runs, printing by lithography is increasingly attractive; it means that both line draw-

ings and half-tone illustrations can be included on any page of the book. But for most non-fiction books of a technical nature line drawings will be more appropriate – no matter how the book is printed.

(5) Most line illustrations in non-fiction books will be diagrams. They should be clear and simple, and not cluttered with inappropriate detail. They should fill the space available and be well, but not excessively, labelled. As well as straightforward representations, flow-charts, graphs, bar charts and pie charts make excellent diagrammatic illustrations.

(6) You may be asked to produce line drawings (without lettering) yourself, or the publisher may agree to accept rough sketches – 'roughs'. In either case, the drawings need to be accurate, clear and properly scaled to permit reduced size reproduction.

(7) Most half-tone illustrations will be black and white photographs; ensure that these are sharp, large enough, well contrasted, and filled with the subject. (And, of course, ensure that no essential heads or feet are cut off – and who can say which are non-essentials?)

(8) Illustrations should be sorted into numerical order and safely packed, not mixed up with, or interleaved in, the typescript, for delivery to the publisher. The publisher will also require copies of a carefully prepared list of captions.

8

Preparing the typescript

The place for originality is in your writing – not in preparing the final typescript. There is one acceptable way in which to present your work to your publisher; there is no room here for innovation. You must present your work in the form that is most convenient for the publisher and the printer.

But first, is your book ready to be typed – or finally typed, if you drafted on a typewriter? Now is the time, the right time, almost the last chance, to check that you still like what you have written. Re-read your finished draft in its entirety, not paragraph by paragraph as you read when you polished, nor even chapter by chapter. Lock yourself away one evening and read it right through as you would a novel.

Check for consistency. Did you say, in chapter 1, something like '. . . as explained more fully in chapter 0.'? And did you pick this up in the later chapter? If not, do something: take out the initial allusion or insert the later explanation. Read the draft as one coming new to the book. Does it really grab you? It should make even you say, to yourself, 'That's good, I'd buy that book'.

If you are going to let friends and colleagues read your book critically, it *must* be at this stage, rather than in proof. You could perhaps type it for them, as long as you are prepared to retype finally. In considering others' comments though, welcome advice of factual errors but beware opinions. Remember that the first camel was a horse designed by a committee.

Not only must your draft be ready for typing, so must everything else. When you deliver the typescript to the publisher he wants it all – main text, illustrations, captions, preliminary pages (title pages, contents page, preface, acknowledgements), appendixes, bibliographies – the lot, in one batch. If you deliver the whole package short of one chapter, you might just as well not bother. The typescript will just have to sit and wait for the missing part – and parts can get lost. The consequences of an incomplete typescript are a frustrated publisher and a reduced opinion of you. And if delivery of the final part is after the agreed delivery date, this may prejudice the whole production timetable.

Typing

By referring above to 'typescript' rather than 'manuscript', I hope I have made the point that the manuscript has to be typed. (The words are otherwise commonly interchangeable.) There can hardly be a publisher anywhere in the world who would now accept a handwritten manuscript. There are no two ways about it. It *must* be typed.

It should not be necessary to say it, but ensure also that the typewriter has a standard – *pica* or *elite* – type face. Do not use a typewriter with a type like handwriting, or all capitals, or any other gimmickry.

Who is to do the typing? I strongly advise you to type your manuscript yourself if you possibly can. Typing is not a desperately difficult skill to master – and if you hope to continue in the writing field it is essential to learn it. You do not need to be very good or very fast – correction paper is a godsend. The object is not to prepare immaculate work, though this would be a bonus, but to produce an easily readable, clear, text.

The great advantage of do-it-yourself typing is the extra opportunity for thought. As you slowly type the final text, you will inevitably notice phrases that are less fluent than you would like. If you are the typist, you can sort them out. If you are not, you cannot.

But some people will never be willing or able to do their own typing. A nearest-and-dearest, or an acquiescent secretary, is the next best thing, but he, or more probably, she must type it the way *you* specify, not the way she prefers.

The whole book manuscript must be typed on one side only of good quality A4 (297 x 210 mm) paper. It *must* be double-spaced throughout. Do *not* type, for instance, quotations or inset material single-spaced, as is sometimes done. There must be good margins on all four sides: 40–50 mm on the left side and 25 mm at top, bottom and right side are the minima. This space is required for editor's and printer's instructions and notes. Figure 9.1 on page 124, shows a typical page of typescript – after the publisher has edited it.

It will help the publisher if you can keep the lines of type as near as possible the same length throughout and maintain a constant number of lines per page. Such consistency facilitates word-counting and book-page-estimating. As a matter of interest, a page of typescript contains around 250 words and a printed page, without illustrations, contains about 400 words – but obviously, this depends on the size of the printed type.

Start each new chapter with a fresh page. Type chapter number and chapter title in capitals about six or seven centimetres down from the top of the page. Start the actual text a further four or five centimetres below that. Type headings in capitals only and subheadings in capitals and lower case, where the layout hierarchy requires it. I have already said though, that I recommend only one level of headings 'below' chapter titles, and I use initial capitals and lower case letters for these. Type headings and sub-headings starting flush with the left margin and allow a double-double space above and below them. Be consistent in this.

Indent the start of each paragraph and leave a double-double space between them. Reserve underlining exclusively for words that you wish to be printed in *italic* in the final book. This applies to headings and sub-headings as well: mark their weight in the margin, Ⓐ, Ⓑ or Ⓒ.

Tables should not be typed as they come in the text, unless they are very small – a few lines only. Ensure that you refer to the table in the text, by number, as for an illustration, and then type the table on a separate sheet of typescript. Insert the page containing the table – and nothing else – immediately after the page on which reference is made to it. (Number tables in the same way as illustrations – by chapter, that is, table 1.1, table 1.2, etc.) As far as possible all tables should have titles. Avoid vertical lines dividing columns – space looks better and is cheaper to print.

Consistency is perhaps the most important quality that a copy-editor (see chapter 9) will look for. Be consistent in such things as:

- use of capitals: in general use capitals sparingly. (Say 'a duke' – but 'the Duke of Norfolk'.)
- use of -ise spelling: use 'rationalise' rather than 'rationalize'.
- use of punctuation: omit full-stops within groups of initials and after abbreviations, for example WHO, MP, Mr, Lt-Col Smith. (When an unfamiliar abbreviation is first used it is often worth writing it in full, followed by the abbreviation in parentheses.)
- use of per cent: use separate words, not percent, and precede by a number, for example, 25 per cent. In tables and notes, the abbreviation % may be used to save space, but not normally in the text.
- use of quotation marks: single marks for speech or quotations; double marks for quotations within quotations.

Most publishers have what they call their *house style* which will include most of the above, which are commonly agreed; they will often have other idiosyncrasies.

In the absence of specific advice from the publisher and/or if in doubt, there are few better sources of advice than the *Authors' & Printers' Dictionary* by F Howard Collins (Oxford University Press). This can usefully be supplemented by *Hart's Rules for Compositors and Readers at the University Press Oxford* (Oxford University Press). Originally compiled by Horace Hart, Printer to the University in 1893, Hart's Rules, as the book is known, has been revised again and again, through at least 38 editions: it is an invaluable guide to good writing practice.

Logistics

Before starting to type a book, a new typewriter ribbon is strongly advised: otherwise, unnoticed, it will wear out, become too faint, before you finish. (And I have once again blessed my *Authors' & Printers' Dictionary* which says quite clearly 'feint ruled, *use* fai-' – whereas the *Concise Oxford Dictionary* offers the option of either usage.) A nylon typewriter ribbon will give a crisper appearance than a cotton one.

Check the type-face too, for cleanliness. You are going to make two carbon copies of the whole typescript; the second copy must not be too fuzzy. The publisher will usually insist on the original plus one carbon copy. And every writer, since Carlyle lost the one-and-only copy of his story of the French Revolution, keeps a copy for himself. You will need it over and over again.

Still thinking about materials, you need paper and carbon paper. Buy a ream (500 sheets) of about 70 g/m^2 (or gsm) – that is, medium-heavy weight – white A4 typing paper, and two reams of *bank* (about 45 gsm) paper of the same size, for the carbon copies. I use white bank paper for the publisher's carbon copy and yellow paper for mine. Using yellow paper for my set makes separation of the copies easier. On no account though should you send the publisher a set of coloured carbon copies: he wants white paper.

To ensure good copies, use good carbon paper – I prefer carbon film – and change it frequently. I exchange first and second carbon 'papers' after each page of typing and at the same time, turn them top to bottom. After about thirty pages of typing I discard the two sheets of carbon. Longer use is false economy.

Number each of the typewritten pages in the main body of the book consecutively throughout, not by chapter. The numbers should be in the top right-hand corner of each page – not at the bottom. My practice is initially to number only my yellow carbon copies, stacking away the other two copies, in proper order and paper-clipped by chapter, but un-numbered. This practice allows me to adjust the page numbering, should I revise after typing, without resorting to the conventional 29A, 29B, etc. on the original. Finally, of course, I ensure that my yellow copies are numbered precisely the same as the top copies – the copy-editor can easily send a query about 'para 2 on folio 125'. (Publishers refer to the typed pages as *folios*, to differentiate them from the book's pages.)

Corrections

Eventually, you will come to the end of the typing task. You will have three piles of typed pages: the immaculate (more-or-less) top copy, the white carbon copy, and your own yellow copy. The yellow pages will be numbered consecutively from 1 to 180 or so. And you still have to prepare and type the preliminary pages and the caption sheets. More about the prelims later, but do not number them in the same sequence as the text.

Punch filing holes in the yellow pages and bind them in a file. Sit down and read it all through again: check for missing lines, typing errors, spelling errors, factual errors, poor English, missing cross-references and major omissions of logic. This really is your last chance – and by now you should not find many errors. Inevitably though, something will be wrong and have to be changed. Perhaps like me, you have to get your employer's blessing on what you have written – he may ask for changes. Mark all changes, in ink, on your yellow copy. Use this, eventually, as a master from which to amend the two sets of white paper pages.

Make corrections boldly and clearly. If the error or correction is small – a figure, a letter, or a single word – I use typists' correction fluid (Liquid Paper or Snopake) on the two white copies. But beware: correction fluid can wear off with excessive handling, permitting both letters to show through. It may be better to cross out neatly and write or type the correction above.

If the amendment is a few lines long, this may be typed above the crossed-out lines or on a strip of paper which is then *glued* (not stapled, pinned, clipped, or cellotaped) to the original. Longer amendments – either the same length as the original or longer, which necessitate a small part being typed at one-and-a-half spacing – should be typed on half a sheet, the balance of the original being stuck to it, or vice-versa. On no account permit the resultant made-up page to be other than standard A4 size. And never, *never*, NEVER make alterations that stick out from the side, or worse, run down the side, of the paper. Best of all, retype one or two whole pages, taking in corrections and additions. You can use more pages than you replace and you need not fill the pages. Having only numbered the yellow pages these can be renumbered to accommodate the extras. Then the top copies can be numbered from 1 straight through to the end, without recourse to 29A, 29B, etc. (If you have to stop a correction/insertion far from the foot of a page, run a diagonal line from end of typing to foot of page, to ensure that the printer realises that the text continues.)

I would now go through the typescript – yellow pages first in case I get it wrong – and make the following marginal notes, in ink:

- 'weight' of chapter title and other headings and sub-headings – by Ⓐ, Ⓑ, Ⓒ, etc., A being the heaviest weight.
- preferred location of illustrations and tables. I usually mark these with F 1.3→, or T 2.2→opposite the nearest space between paragraphs after the first textual reference, but sometimes other locations are better and need identifying. Not all publishers ask for these illustration and table locations to be identified – they automatically insert them as soon as possible after the first textual reference – but it does no harm. The printer will place illustrations and tables as near as possible to where you suggest: actual placing is his, and the book designer's, job.

Prelims and end matter

The main body of the book typed, think now of the peripheral pages. The first of these are the preliminary pages – known as the *prelims.* These pages, usually numbered in books in small roman figures, consist of:

page (i) *Half-title.* Always a right-hand page: it contains the title only.

page (ii) *Half-title verso.* The reverse (verso) of the half-title, thus always a left-hand page. Here, subject to the agreement of your publisher, might be listed other books you have written. It might also be used to list books by other writers in the same series.

page (iii) *Title-page.* Always a right-hand page. It carries the full title, with sub-title, if any, the name of the author (with academic qualifications if desired) and the publisher's imprint, or his name and abbreviated address.

page (iv) *Title-page verso.* The reverse of the title-page, again, always a left-hand page. This page is used for legal and bibliographical requirements. It is here that you will look for the British Library Cataloguing in Publication Data that we referred to in chapter 2. If space is short, any dedication – which should always be as brief as possible – is also accommodated on the title-verso. With more space, a dedication is given a right-hand page of its own, with a blank verso.

page (v)+ *Contents.* Conventionally, these begin on a right-hand page. Details of contents preparation are below.

From the contents page onward the prelims vary from book to book. You should agree any special requirements with your publisher.

When preparing the typescript for delivery to the publisher, you should prepare typed prelims as above. Look at any book for a model. Type the half-title, the half-title verso, the title-page as you wish them to be – even though they may be changed. I usually provide a sheet merely marked © Gordon Wells 198 . . for the title-page verso; its purpose is more to keep the numbering right than anything else.

The contents page(s) should be prepared from the typescript. They should consist, for each chapter, of the chapter number and title, often followed by a precise repetition of the wording of each of the headings you have used in the text. Follow the list of chapters with the titles of the end matter – see below. Once typed, it is my practice to insert, in pencil, on the top copy of the contents page, the page (folio) numbers against each chapter title. These will obviously have to be corrected when the pages are printed, but folio numbers are a convenience when editing.

A preface is sometimes required. In this book its purpose is filled by the 'blurb' on the back cover. The preface is the book's shop window: it is what is read by the casual bookshop browser and – importantly – by the book reviewer. It is the place to explain the purpose of the book: why it is special. Much of the material that you prepared (chapter 3) for the statement of objectives would be appropriate for inclusion here. Your statement of objectives sold the idea to the publisher: it should serve as well for the reader. If you need to acknowledge the assistance of others, personal thanks can be included at the end of the preface. More formal acknowledgements should be separated, to follow the preface.

Contents pages and prefaces should, of course, be typed double-spaced. It is useful to provide the publisher with a list of illustrations, or as suggested in chapter 7, a clearly identified extra photocopy of, and in addition to, the caption list. Sometimes the printed prelims will include a list of illustrations, but this is unusual. Do not number preliminary pages in the same sequence as the main folios – instead use small roman figures, as for the printed pages.

The *end matter* of a book is less formalised than the prelims. It will consist at most of *Appendixes, Notes* (replacing footnotes), *Bibliography* (or Reading List), and *Index*. All except the index should be sent to the publisher with the rest of the book material. And all should be typed double-spaced. Continue the page numbering of the main body of the text to include the end matter.

There are conventions for the preparation of the bibliography and of references in the notes. It is usual to refer to the books by, in order: author's name; book title, underlined for italic, and not in quotes; edition, where relevant; and place of publication, publisher, and date, all in parentheses. In notes, where references are not listed alphabetically, the author's name is written conventionally; in a bibliography, books should be listed in alphabetical order of author, whose name is then printed surname first, followed by first name (preferred) or initials. In reference notes the relevant page number(s) in the book should be cited at the end.

Delivery to the publisher

All of your material is now typed. All the pages are numbered consecutively, with prelims numbered in a separate sequence.

You have three complete copies – your own yellow pages and the original plus the white copy for the publisher. All of the illustrations are ready – either as roughs or finished drawings – and full captions have been written and typed. Any necessary copyright approvals have been granted. Everything is complete and ready.

Separate the publisher's copies of the typescript into chapters: fold a small piece of (yellow) paper over the top left corner of the folios in each chapter and secure with a paper clip. Do *not* use a pin, or a staple; do *not* punch a hole through the pages and use a Treasury tag. The paper clip is for convenience, it can – and will – be discarded. Meanwhile, it will not have speared the inevitably haemophiliac reader, nor caused the pages to tear when it is removed. Group together the whole of the top copy and put the papers in the box in which the paper was supplied, or in a simple document wallet. Repeat for the carbon copy. Identify both boxes or wallets on the outside: WIDGETS – GORDON WELLS – ORIGINAL/CARBON.

My custom is now to list the contents of each package – which will be identical apart from the original illustrations – for security. This is not absolutely essential, but it makes *me* feel better. My list would say something like:

HOW TO WIDGET – GORDON WELLS
Prelims: 10 folios numbered (i) to (x)
Text and end matter: comprising 10 chapters and a bibliography in 193 folios
(Index to follow)

Illustrations (in separate envelope within *original* wallet only):
10 line illustrations – roughs for redrawing
5 black-and-white photographic prints
*10 'word illustrations' – to be set as text, but 'boxed'
*List of 25 captions – on 10 folios lettered A to K.

*These in *duplicate* wallet also.

NOTE

(1) Preferred illustration and table locations are indicated in LH margin of original copy (F1.1/T1.1)

(2) Chapter headings are marked in margin of original copy as Chapter heading.
Sub-headings in text (one level only) marked as Ⓐ.

Whenever possible I prefer to deliver the whole typescript package by hand. Delivery must of course be on or before your deadline. You agreed to work to this date. If you were not able to meet the deadline, even by working nights, you should have forewarned the publisher and agreed a revised date. Depending on my relationship with my editor I may either telephone or write to warn of delivery. But however preceded, I merely deliver the typescript as a package to the publisher's reception desk. I do not seek to discuss it with the editor at this stage. He will get in touch with me as and when he needs to. Everything necessary should have been included in either the 'list of contents', the material itself, or a covering letter.

If I have to despatch the material by post, I send original and copy typescripts in two separate envelopes, both by registered post. And I ask the publisher to acknowledge receipt, supplying him with a stamped addressed envelope for the purpose.

Starting on the index

Immediately after I have despatched the manuscript I start on the index. I go through my yellow copy of the manuscript and underline in *coloured* ink (to differentiate from italicisation) everything that I think should be indexed. Where a single word or two-word phrase best expresses the content, but does not itself appear in the text, then I write this word or phrase, in coloured ink, at the top of the page.

By their nature, virtually every heading within a chapter should be marked for indexing; so too (and often overlooked) should diagrammatic illustrations, check lists, and the like.

I then mark sheets of A4 paper with the letters of the alphabet. I use both sides of the paper and group the less used letters, IJK, PQ, UV, XYZ, together. The ten sheets are stapled together. Now I can start indexing.

I work right through the manuscript and write – on the appropriate letter-headed sheet – each index item and its folio number. Had I identified an item 'Index preparation', I would enter this on the lettered sheets under both I and P (for 'Preparation of Index'). Once every underlined item is entered on to the working sheets it is then necessary to put the entries for each letter in order and, where appropriate, to group entries together.

There will be perhaps twenty or so entries to each letter. I go through the entries repeatedly, muttering to myself as I do, 'Ra, Ra, Ra, – nothing; Rb, Rc, Rd – impossible; Re, Re – reviewers – folio 45; . . . etc.' As I put the entries in order, I number them to the left of the page. I treat all letters in the index item as of equal weight and ignore word-splits. See the example, which also shows how the ordered list is eventually typed out.

Example of the listing, ordering and typing of index items.

Ordering	As listed: (folio)	As typed
4	word-budget, 54, 57, 64, F5.1	Within-chapter word-budget,
3	within-chapter word-budget, 57	Word-budget,
5	word processing equipment, 62	Word processing equipment,
7	words, counting, 64, 74, F5.1	Word-splits,
8	words, short, 73	Words
9	words, simple and familiar, 75	counting,
6	word-splits, 113	short,
	...	simple and familiar,
	...	

The index can now be typed. As for all other parts of the book, type it double-spaced – with double-double space between letters – on white A4 paper, with at least two carbon copies. Once again, the setting out is of particular importance. Each entry should be typed on a separate line. Indent all sub-entries by two typewriter spaces and separate the entry from what will eventually be the page number, with a comma. Do NOT type the folio numbers. Leave space for later completion, on receipt of page proofs. No punctuation is required at the end of each entry. Should you need to index sub-sub-entries – which will confuse the reader and should be avoided – indent these a further two typewriter spaces. Number the typed pages of the index I1, I2, I3, etc.

Some publishers welcome receipt of the carbon copy of the index with folio numbers pencilled in. Certainly I always pencil folio numbers for each entry into my own, yellow, copy of the index. Other publishers do not want the index in advance at all, but *all* publishers want the completed original plus carbon copy as soon as possible after page proof stage. I usually compromise and make three carbon copies, one of which, with folio numbers only, I send to the publisher as early as possible. That way I can still provide an original plus carbon copy index immediately I get the page proofs. We will look at how to complete the index in the next chapter.

Summary

(1) Ensure that the draft is complete and as correct as you can get, before you start typing. Typing is essential for all manuscripts: publishers will not consider hand-written work. Fancy type-faces should be avoided.

(2) Typing your book yourself provides an opportunity for further polishing, as you type.

(3) Type on good quality white A4 paper, double-spaced, with good margins, making two carbon copies of everything. Keep words per line and lines per page generally

consistent throughout. Number pages (folios) in top right corner, consecutively throughout, not by chapter.

(4) Make corrections to the typescript if you must – a few are acceptable – but make them clear. Do not scribble amendments up the side margin: if the printer has to turn the page round every now and then, he will charge more for the work. Retype whole pages for other than minor alterations.

(5) Type tables on separate pages. Mark preferred locations of tables and illustrations in left margins (T1.1→; F1.1→). Similarly identify 'weight' of sub-headings by marginal notes.

(6) Keep prelims separate from main text. Number folios in small roman figures. The contents page should include (accurate) chapter titles and – often – the headings within chapters. End-matter folios should continue the numbering of the main text. There are detailed conventions for setting out references.

(7) Deliver original and one carbon copy of all material to the publisher – by hand if possible, but impersonally. It helps to list what is being delivered. It is essential that you deliver on time.

(8) Prepare the index from your copy of the typescript. Type it double-spaced as with everything else. Perhaps let the publisher have a carbon copy of the index with the folio numbers marked in pencil. Mark folio numbers on your own copy of the index. Later, insert the book page numbers, from the page proofs, into the original index.

9

From typescript to book

You have delivered your completed manuscript (typescript) – your newborn brain-child – to the publisher. What does he do with it?

The commissioning or sponsoring editor to whom you have delivered the typescript will first of all have it read. He may well read it himself, but more important, he will have it read by one or more people, commissioned by the publisher, who know your subject well. These may or may not be the same readers who gave their views on your sample chapters. Their task now is to ensure that your work is correct and is interesting to those in the appropriate specialist field. They may notice errors of fact which you have overlooked. They may find a technical explanation confusing, and if it is not clear to an expert, it will certainly not do for a 'beginner-reader'.

After the readers have reported to your editor, he will decide what weight to put on their comments. Probably he will refer the readers' comments to you for your views. He may ask – or you may offer – for part of the book to be rewritten. Usually, this part is small and is most often due to a need for further clarification. Do not be unduly perturbed about the need for some rewriting – as long as it is not half the book. Even if it is that much, you should still comply.

Alternatively, you will need to convince the editor that you are right and both he and the readers are wrong.

Put aside any ideas of literary pride. Leave such feelings for the 'better' novelists and poets. Your object is to have your own published book on your bookshelf, and to make some money from it. If a partial rewrite will help achieve that, start rewriting. All of the publisher's requirements at this or any other stage in production, will be intended solely to improve the saleability of your book. You are not a literary genius, or you would not be reading this book. You are not perfect, you are human: humans make mistakes, sometimes big ones. Accept these facts and treat the readers' and editor's comments and requests as helpful and necessary.

At some stage round about now – depending on the terms of your agreement – you may be eligible for, and receive, an advance on your royalties, as already mentioned in chapter 4. The better contracts – from the author's point of view – provide for the advance *on delivery* of the manuscript; publishers often, and understandably, prefer to pay the advance *on their acceptance* of the manuscript. Watch for this point in the agreement, at which we shall look further in chapter 10. Whenever you get that attractive-looking cheque, it is a further positive assurance of the progress of your book.

By now, one way or another, the commissioning or sponsoring editor is satisfied with your manuscript. That is his task at this stage – to satisfy himself about the *content* of your work. He can now send the original of your masterpiece off to a colleague – the *copy-editor.* Meanwhile, the carbon copy goes to one or more printers for estimates of production costs.

The other main use for the carbon copy manuscript that you have given the publisher, is to act as a reference copy in his office when the edited original has finally gone for printing. If your book has possibilities for sales in other countries, the publisher may also wish to show the carbon copy to foreign publishers.

Copy-editing

The copy-editor is not concerned with the content so much as with the 'quality'. The copy-editor's task is to check and 'polish' your English; to check for consistency of style both within your writing and with the publisher's *house style* (mentioned already, in chapter 8); and to prepare the typescript for printing – which is explained below.

The average non-fiction writer – and for all I know, the average novelist too – has a love–hate relationship with the average copy-editor. But of course none of us, nor our associates, is 'average'. My problem springs directly from my sometimes over-casual style of writing: I seem fated to pair up with over-pedantic copy-editors. But I have nothing but praise for the way they sort out the worst of my grammatical 'howlers'. My punctuation habits have improved immeasurably since I started paying attention to the way that the copy-editors corrected it. And I have had many a split-infinitive repaired by a kindly copy-editor. (I have also experienced an unpopular copy-editor who expunged every 'and' and 'but' with which I had occasionally – and deliberately – started sentences in one book.)

Setting aside all facetious – part-facetious anyway – criticism of copy-editors, they do an essential job, and one for which all writers should be thankful. You cannot expect them to be expert in your subject though. It is up to *you* to ensure that the copy-editor does not, unwittingly and while improving your English, change the sense of what you are saying. Insist therefore that the manuscript comes back to you after editing and before going off to the printer. But when you get it, deal with it very quickly, overnight if possible.

The other part of the copy-editor's task is to prepare the typescript for printing. This entails marking it with instructions for the printer: the best-looking layout of a printed page is not necessarily the same as a well-laid-out page of typescript. As an example, most typists – correctly – indent the start of each paragraph by some five or six spaces: on the printed page it is customary to indent by the equivalent of about two spaces – one 'em'. Similarly, while two or three short items listed beneath each other will look good in typescript, the copy-editor may decide that they will look better in print if run on, as a long sentance. Even when lists are retained – as in this book, for example – they will almost certainly not be inset to the extent that they are in my typescript. Figure 9.1 shows a page of the typescript for this book – from chapter 8 – after editing.

Printers' terms

The instructions to the printer will also include comments about type size. This may have been pre-agreed for the bulk of the text but inevitably there will be some material that will have to be set in a different size of type. (Table headings, or footnotes – which of course you will not be using – are typical uses of smaller type.) While not of great importance to the author, it will help his appreciation of the production task if he understands the meaning of some printing terms. Halfway down page iv of the prelims of this book is the phrase, 'Typeset in 11/12pt Baskerville'. It is interesting to understand the meaning of this.

All type is measured in terms of *points.* One point is approximately 1/72 inch and a *pica* is 12 points (12/72 inch or 1/6 inch). Pica, or 12-point type is the largest type size in common use. A point is the size of the pica full-stop. The type size is not the measurement of any letter, it is the vertical space required to accommodate the type body: it is the equivalent of the distance from the base of one line of type to the base of the line above or below. In 12-point type therefore there are almost exactly six lines to the inch. (One point = 0.351 mm or 0.013837 inch: 72 points = 25.272 mm or 0.9962 inch.)

When you see 'set in 10-point . . . ' this means that the

103

Tables should not be typed as they come in the text, unless they are very small - a few lines only. Ensure that you refer to the table in the text, by number, as for an illustration, and then type the table on a separate sheet of typescript. Insert the page containing the table - and nothing else - immediately after the page on which reference is made to it. (Number tables in the same way as illustrations - by chapter, eg Table 1.1, Table 3.2, etc.) As far as possible all tables should have titles, and avoid vertical lines dividing columns - space looks better and is cheaper to print.

Consistency is perhaps the most important quality that a copy-editor (see Chapter 9) will look for. Be consistent in such things as:

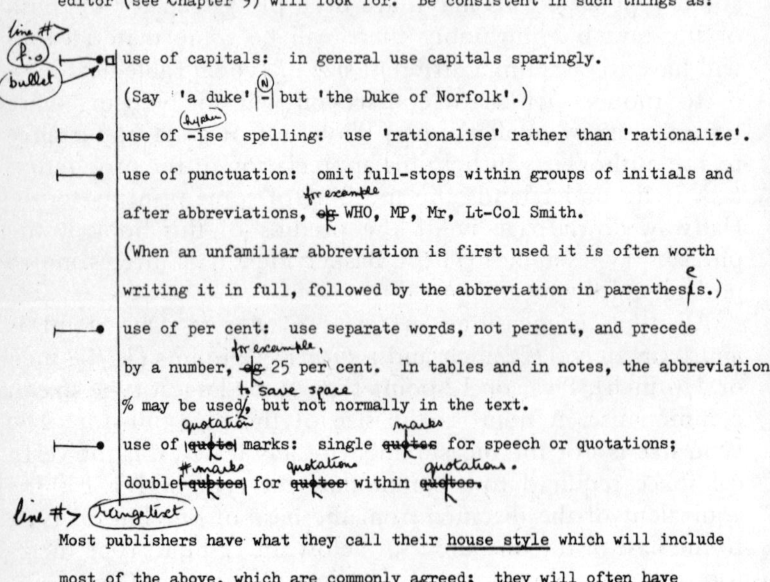

use of capitals: in general use capitals sparingly.
(Say 'a duke' - but 'the Duke of Norfolk'.)

use of -ise spelling: use 'rationalise' rather than 'rationalize'.

use of punctuation: omit full-stops within groups of initials and after abbreviations, eg WHO, MP, Mr, Lt-Col Smith.
(When an unfamiliar abbreviation is first used it is often worth writing it in full, followed by the abbreviation in parenthesis.)

use of per cent: use separate words, not percent, and precede by a number, eg 25 per cent. In tables and in notes, the abbreviation % may be used, but not normally in the text.

use of quote marks: single quotes for speech or quotations; double quotes for quotes within quotes.

Most publishers have what they call their <u>house style</u> which will include most of the above, which are commonly agreed; they will often have other idiosyncrasies.

Fig 9.1 A page (a *folio*) of the typescript of chapter 8 of this book after editing. Note the author's setting-out of the typescript and the copy-editor's changes and instructions to the printer.

letters are set on type-metal ten points tall – that is, roughly 10 x 1/72 inch. When you see '10 point on 12' (or 10/12) this means 10-point letters set within 12-point vertical spacing – for easier reading. The 'Baskerville' on page iv relates to the design of the type-face: there are many different designs. The choice of type-face for your own book will be made by the publisher from the ones the chosen printer has available. The choice is no concern of yours.

The pica is the standard vertical measure: the *en* and the *em* are the units used in measuring the width (length) of a line of type. The *en* is half of an *em*. The *em* is the square of any size of type: thus a 12 point em is 12 points wide and a 10 point em is 10 points wide. It is customary to measure line lengths in terms of 12 point ems (picas). Type size and the typographical terms associated with it are illustrated in Figure 9.2.

Eventually, the work of the copy-editor will be complete – as Figure 9.1 – and you will have made a quick check to ensure that no errors have been 'edited in'. The work now goes to the printer to be typeset.

Proofs

Within not too long a time – but always longer than you think – you will get your *proofs* for correction. Proofs are produced on poor quality paper but they should be accurately typeset. They can be galley proofs (*galleys*) or page proofs. A galley is not divided up into pages nor are illustrations included. Each galley usually contains about enough material for three pages of the book. Increasingly though, unless books are very complicated, they go straight into what used to be the second proof stage – *page proofs*. These are what the name implies, proofs of what the actual pages will look like. Sometimes spaces are left for incomplete illustrations – of which there should be none – otherwise the proofs should be complete, except for the index. (The proofs may not all arrive in your letter box at the same time: they will probably

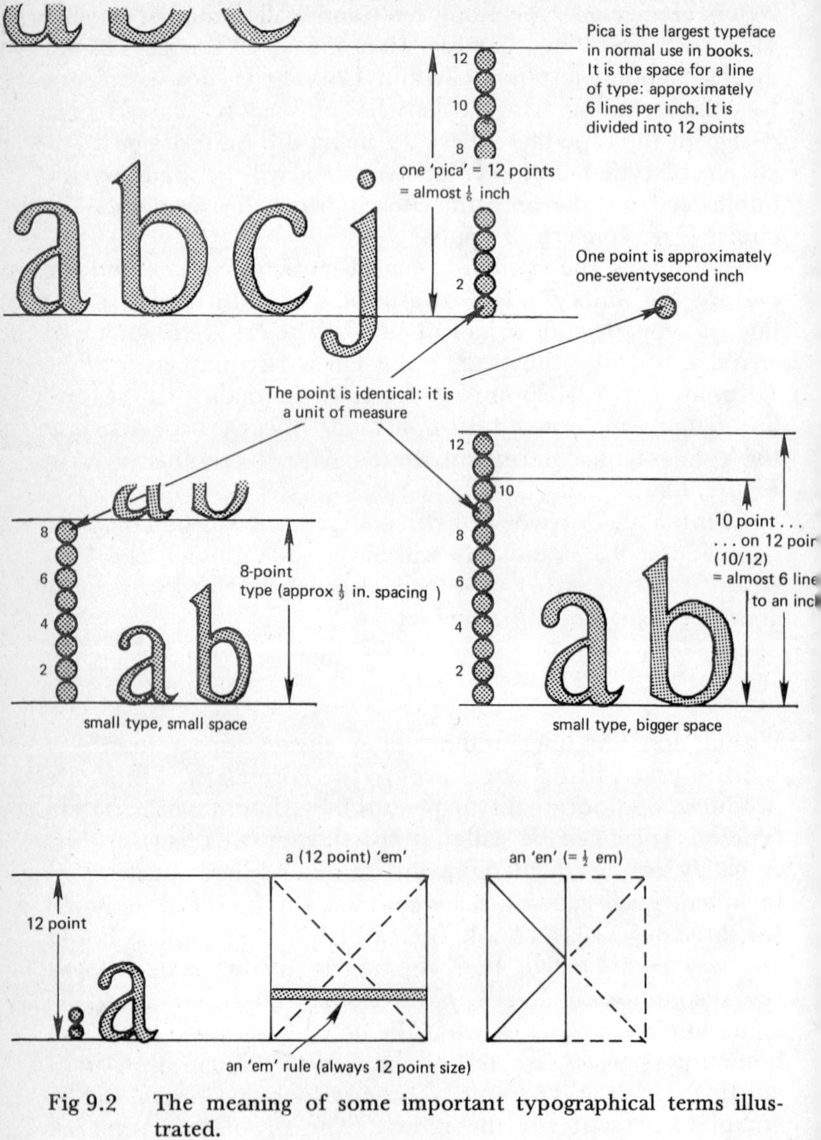

Pica is the largest typeface in normal use in books. It is the space for a line of type: approximately 6 lines per inch. It is divided into 12 points

12
10
8
one 'pica' = 12 points
= almost $\frac{1}{6}$ inch
2

One point is approximately one-seventysecond inch

The point is identical: it is a unit of measure

8
6
4
2
8-point type (approx $\frac{1}{9}$ in. spacing)
small type, small space

12
10
8
6
4
2
10 point . . .
. . . on 12 poir
(10/12)
= almost 6 line
to an inc
small type, bigger space

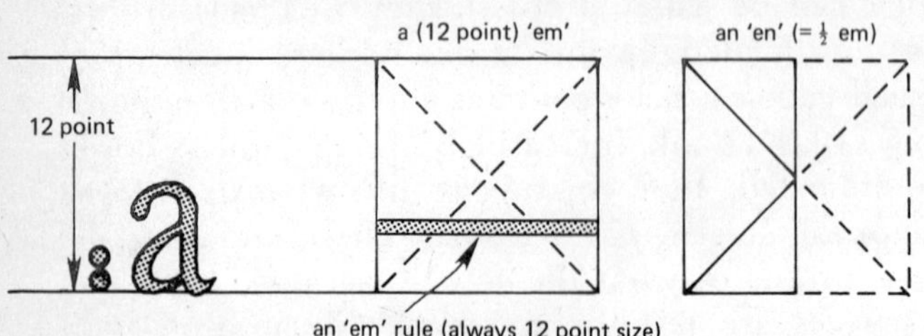

Fig 9.2 The meaning of some important typographical terms illustrated.

be sent to you in batches. You should deal with them in the same way, without waiting for all to arrive.)

Proofs are produced for the purpose of being checked. They are not a device for improving your explanations or changing your mind. That is important enough to warrant repeating more strongly:

PROOFS ARE FOR CORRECTING:
NOT FOR MIND-CHANGING

If you change just one letter or insert a punctuation mark in a line, not only will that line have to be reset – often expensively, by hand – but a word may have to be carried over to the next line. And that can easily have a 'knock-on' effect for several lines. If the first line is at either end of a page, the 'knock-on' effect could even mean changes on two pages. And all for the sake of a punctuation mark! It is seldom worth it. Changing whole words or sentences can be progressively worse – and more costly. If there are author's errors – real errors, not 'cosmetic' ones – though, these should of course be corrected. See below for advice on economical correction techniques.

You will usually be sent two sets of proofs: let us assume that they will be page proofs. One set will be annotated; the other will be unmarked and may be labelled 'author's set'. Whether labelled or not, the unmarked set is for you to retain. You may also be sent the annotated original typescript, now well-thumbed, for comparison.

The marked set and the typescript have to be returned to the publisher, for the printer. The marked set will probably have been checked and corrected by the printer's proof-reader, possibly also by the copy-editor. The printer will have marked his own errors and any queries in green. You are expected to check for more printer's errors and particularly to answer his queries; you may also have to make a few textual corrections. (We are all human, some mistakes will always slip through.) You should mark the printing errors that you find, in red ink: mark your own alterations and instructions in black or blue.

The printer will not charge for correcting his own mistakes but he will certainly bill the publisher for yours. If the cost is excessive the publisher will in turn deduct the cost of excess corrections from your royalty account. One of the clauses in your agreement will allow the publisher to bill you for author's alterations costing more than a specified percentage of the original cost of composition. Do not be misled into thinking that this means you can change that proportion of the text. The original typesetting is done as an on-going machine process – all corrections have to be made individually and partly by hand. They cost far more to set than the original work, and this cost is, in turn, increased by the extra handling and proofreading.

Proofreading requires careful application, to spot the errors. You, the author, can spot omitted paragraphs particularly, far more easily than can printer's readers or publisher's editors. But beware! Because you wrote the book and know what it says, you may not read the proofs as carefully as you should. You can do it on your own, but it pays to enlist the help of another person to read the proofs to you, for checking against the original. Proofreading also requires the use of standard correction marks. These are shown in appendix 2: they should be learnt. Use only standard marks: non-standard marks will not be understood and may either be ignored or misinterpreted.

One of the most important things to note about the task of proofreading is the need to make the marks in order in one or other of the margins, as well as in the text. The printer runs his eyes down the margins; he does not look at the text until a marginal mark indicated a need for action. After each marginal mark, make an oblique stroke /: in this way several corrections can be indicated within a single line.

Make all corrections on the marked set and answer all queries – briefly. The printer does not want to read a long explanation. Watch out particularly for missing page numbers and references in the text. Complete these now, in black.

We have already acknowledged that no matter how you try to perfect your manuscript before it is delivered, some error or fault will slip through. (This is sometimes known as Murphy's Law.) These errors must of course be corrected at proof stage. But do it economically. If you have to rewrite a line, a sentence, or a paragraph, make the new one as near the same length as possible. Ideally, count the characters – space, letters, numerals and punctuation marks – and make the new material exactly the same length. If you need to cut words out, try to put in some innocuous verbal padding of the same length. If you need to add words, look for some padding to take out.

Above all, the proofs must be read, checked and corrected, both carefully and quickly. Do it yourself. This is NOT the time to send the proofs to a colleague for his opinion. That should have been done before you delivered the manuscript. Burn the midnight oil over the proofs. Get them right and do it quickly. Finally, before you return the marked set (and the original typescript) to the publisher, mark up your own set of proofs. You will need them again. Figure 9.3 is a useful check list of things to consider when proofreading.

Completing the index

If you are following the procedure that I have recommended, you will already be well on the way to completing the index for your book. We started work on this in chapter 8. Now is the time to complete it. The index is an important part of a non-fiction book: it helps the reader to find his way *back* into the subject. (Similarly, we can think of the contents page as helping him find his way *in*.) Check that the draft that you prepared and typed from the manuscript still meets with your approval. Because you have been 'apart' from your

1 Ensure that all printer's queries are answered – briefly. (And OK is not an adequate answer: if the answer is *yes*, cross out the question mark: if *no*, cross out the whole query and write in the correction.)

2 Before making an author's correction, convince yourself that it is essential, not just cosmetic. Be particularly chary of changing punctuation marks.

3 Ensure that only standard proof-reading marks are used – and used properly.

4 Insert all previously omitted page, illustration, or chapter numbers in references. Rectify any other ommissions – eg in my typescript for this book I left blank the ISBN number for completion at page proof stage – in chapter 2.

5 Compare, and as far as possible equalise, lengths of inserted and deleted material.

6 Check that there are no passages missing, or – as sometimes happens – repeated.

7 Check that illustrations and text agree – and are appropriately placed and correctly numbered. Check captions too.

8 Check the running headlines – these are often overlooked. Check that they are not transposed, page for page.

9 Check that chapter titles and contents in the prelims agree with those in the text.

10 Check that your handwritten corrections and instructions are legible – unclear corrections will lead to further errors.

Fig 9.3 A proofreading check list

masterpiece while it was at the printers, you can now re-look at the index from a reader's point of view.

Work right through your set of page proofs. Check them page by page with your (yellow) typescript. Underline, in the same coloured ink that you used on the typescript, all of the words or phrases that you have indexed. The end result will be an index-marked page proof set, identical, in this respect, with your index-marked typescript.

Starting on book page 1, and working now on your yellow carbon copy of the index, in which are listed typescript folio numbers, look up the index entry for each underlined item. Work through the yellow manuscript pages at the same time: check the pencilled folio number before crossing it out and substituting the book page number. If there is no corresponding folio number, you may not be looking up the correct index entry – or you made a mistake in preparation. The yellow-copy index pages will gradually all look like this:

00, 00, 00
Statement, objective, ~~00~~, ~~00~~, ~~00~~

(The crossed-out figures are the folio numbers being replaced by the book page numbers.)

The original and one carbon copy of the index will not have had the folio numbers pencilled in. From your yellow 'master' sheets you can now insert the book page numbers into these 'publisher's copies'. It is ideal if you can type in the page numbers – but I usually write them in, VERY CLEARLY. And be sure to get the punctuation right.

The method I have described above and in the previous chapter is the one I use myself. Other advice, particularly specialist advice on indexing, suggests what I consider to be a slower and more complicated method. It may well be more appropriate for longer indexes than I have experienced. My indexes usually have about 350–400 entries.

The classic approach to indexing is to wait for the page proofs and only then, underline index items in these. From these underlined items the classic recommendation is to prepare small cards (perhaps standard 5 inch x 3 inch index cards cut into four) for each entry. The item is written on the card exactly as it will appear in the completed index. Finally, or as each card is completed, the cards are sorted into alphabetical order. From the alphabetically-sorted cards the index can be typed, complete.

Like every other part of the book-production process involving the printers, it is essential that you do not delay in providing the index. Agreements often say things like, 'provide material for the index *promptly*'. Personally, I reckon on being able to send the complete index to the publisher in the same bundle as the final corrected batch of 'marked' page proofs. I suggest that a week after completion of page proofs should be thought of as the latest target date for delivery of the index – to be beaten if at all possible.

The book arrives

It is unlikely that you will receive proofs of the index – the copy-editor will probably check these without bothering you. The next step along the process should be the delivery to you, in advance of publication date, of your six complimentary copies of the finished book. (This may also be the occasion for another part of your advance of royalties.)

Your book! Actually published! You will be eager to show your friends and colleagues. But a word of warning! You receive six free copies to do with as you will, and many of your friends will ask for, and perhaps expect, a free copy. Every copy you give away to someone really interested in its content means a possible sale lost.

Give one copy to an interested relative perhaps, or to your best friend – but only one, and be sure it is really wanted. For the rest, think carefully where they should go. You will want one yourself to thumb through, to note possible improvements for future editions. You may also, if you are like me, want to keep one copy in brand-new condition, to wave in front of friends. (And if you must, lend them your well-thumbed copy, not this one.) If your book relates to your work you may well feel the need, or be required, to give a copy to the firm's library, and/or to the boss. If you were helped in writing it by a colleague, he may have a right to expect a free copy.

Consider just those possibilities; a copy each for the best friend; you, for use; you, for 'posterity'; library and colleague. That only leaves one more free copy. Think before you give it away.

Summary

(1) When delivered to the publisher, your finished manuscript is read by experts. They may suggest that part(s) of the book be rewritten. These suggestions will improve the saleability of your book. Swallow any false pride and rewrite as requested – quickly.
(2) The manuscript now goes to the copy-editor – whose task is to ensure good English and consistency of style, and to instruct the printer on how to set the book.
(3) Eventually the typescript will be converted into print and you will receive proof copies – perhaps galleys, but more likely direct to page proof. Proofs are for correcting – not an opportunity for authors to change their minds. But if you have made a mistake, correct it by all means, and as economically as possible.
(4) Economical corrections at page proof stage mean, as far as possible, equalising characters deleted and characters inserted.
(5) The index, prepared in draft from the typescript folios, can quickly be completed from page proofs annotated identically to the typescript. Overmark the folio numbers on your own copy of the index with book page numbers

and transfer corrected numbers to the original and carbon copy for the publisher. The index should be completed and despatched promptly to the publisher.

(6) You only get six free copies of your book. *Think* before you give them all away.

10
Business matters

Your book is published. For the moment your writing work is done.

So far in this book we have looked at the process of getting the book accepted, written and published. But there are business matters that you will have had to deal with, between the conception and the publication of your book. We can stand back and look at these now. They are important: you will recall that in chapter 1 a professional, that is, commercial, attitude to writing was recommended.

Several times already, in previous chapters, the agreement has been mentioned, with the promise of further comment in this chapter. The agreement is at the hub of the recommended professional attitude.

The importance of the agreement

Most publishers have standard printed forms for their agreements, or contracts, with provision for certain variable parts to be added. Most publishers' agreement forms are basically similar; many are based on a specimen contract produced by The Publishers Association. The legal wording of the 'standard' clauses is fitted to publishing and writing; all that you will get if you ask your solicitor to check it for you is a big bill. (Members of the Society of Authors can have agreements professionally vetted by the Society.) The important aspect of the contract is how it will affect you. Even the standard printed clauses can be varied if you ask for *sensible* variations. Most – but unfortunately not all – publishers treat their authors fairly. Discuss any queries with your commissioning or sponsoring editor.

As far as you – the new writer – are concerned, the most important parts of the agreement are:

- the book length and delivery date,
- the royalty rates and advances,
- the commitment or undertaking to publish.

Before the agreement is prepared by the publisher, you may have the opportunity to discuss these matters with him. If not, he will probably write to you advising what he proposes. There is no reason why you should not write back and seek changes if you wish. It is wise to get the business matters sorted out before the contract is prepared and sent to you for signature.

You will have told the publisher how long you expect the book to be: he will either accept that length or ask for it to be varied. You will reach a compromise and agree on a length. You will then be bound, by your contract, to that length. A small variation will probably be acceptable, a large one will not. We have explained in chapter 5 the importance of working to the agreed length. Warn your editor of any variations in length that you foresee. He may wish to suggest ways of combating your brevity, or more likely, your over-wordiness.

The contract may specify the length in thousands of words plus a number of illustrations, or it may specify a number of book pages, which can usually be translated at 400 words per page. Remember to allow space for the illustrations too in this situation.

It is worth repeating the advice already given in chapter 4 about the importance of the delivery date. You should have discussed this carefully with the publisher. You may think you need twelve months to write your book; he may try to persuade you to do it in six. Once again, you will reach a compromise, which should preferably be a little – but not too much – on the generous side. (A tight deadline is a better spur to an author's productivity than are the intermittent promptings of the muse.) Once agreed, that delivery date will go into the contract: you should adhere to it – or face the (remote) possibility of the book being rejected for lateness.

Royalties and advances

Now the money side – royalties and advances. There are few hard-and-fast rules about authors' payments but many publishers offer an initial royalty rate of 10 per cent of the British published price for home sales of hardback books and 7½ per cent *of the same price* for overseas sales. (The publisher has to offer a further discount to overseas distributors: hence the lower rate.) Books published initially in paperback are commonly paid royalties of 7½ per cent, but 5 per cent is not uncommon on small-profit-margin publications. Similarly, some publishers of hardback books will only offer 7½ per cent on a small-print-run book, particularly if it looks considerably less than a best-seller and/or is unusually expensive to produce.

It is not uncommon for royalty rates to be increased after sales reach a certain figure. This sales figure is usually that at which the publisher will have recouped his original investment. At this sales level royalties usually increase by 2½ per cent. Sometimes there is a second 2½ per cent step. But beware – do not get carried away with dreams of early retirement to a life of Bahaman luxury. Many books never reach sales sufficient to bring them into the increased royalty bracket. The 'royalty jump' is usually set at the size of the initial print run of the book – not all of my books have sold that many. But those that do, provide the 'jam'.

There is a growing pressure from some publishers for royalties to be based on their net receipts rather than on the published price of the book. This is easier for them to calculate and obviates the need for separate rates for overseas sales. It is also particularly appropriate for educational books which are sometimes published without a specific retail price. Because they sell the book at a discount, the publisher's net receipt per copy is obviously less than full price. The royalty rate paid to the author should therefore reflect that lower unit price.

(If the publisher offers bookshops a 35 per cent discount on a marked price of, say, £4.00, his net receipts are £2.60 per copy. A 10 per cent royalty on net receipts of £2.60 equals 26p per copy, which is 6½ per cent of the published price. To achieve the equivalent of a 10 per cent royalty on published price, the publisher would need to pay over 15 per cent on net receipts. But, of course, the discount varies, invalidating any such precise calculation.)

Royalties are paid to the author either once or twice a year. (You get no more money from six-monthly payments, but you do get that warm affluent feeling twice as often.) They are based on sales up to a specified date – differentiating, where appropriate, between home and overseas sales – and paid perhaps three months after that date. The agreement will specify the annual date(s) for assessing sales and for paying the royalties. There is usually a clause that allows the publisher to hold over royalty cheques for very small amounts (less than £5 is common); these are left to accrue and are paid later.

Authors should ask for, if they are not first offered, a payment in advance and on account of the royalties. Few publishers will object to such an advance; it serves the author as a partial surety for publication. The size of the advance varies considerably – I have been paid advances as small as £30 and as big as £300, both extremes on books with similar published prices. Logically, the bigger the advance you can persuade the publisher to pay you, the greater his commitment to push sales to recoup the advance. It is said that an advance could be as much as about fifty per cent of the total royalties likely to be payable on the initial print run. With the technical non-fiction book, by a beginner, that we are considering, I think 25 per cent is the maximum you can hope to get.

The advance against royalties can be paid at any or all of the following stages:

- On signing the contract – that is, before you do much work on the book. Only the best-known writers can expect a really big advance at this stage. But always *try* to get at least a part of the advance 'up front': it reduces any uncertainty about payment on delivery.
- On *delivery* of the manuscript – but publishers sometimes specify that the advance at this stage be 'on *acceptance* of the manuscript'. That qualification can turn the agreement into a 'we'll think some more about your book when you've written it' document – which is of no great value to the author. A writer wants the publisher to commit himself on the basis of the sample chapters and synopsis. This is a reasonable expectation for an experienced writer; the publisher's caution is understandable when he is dealing with a first-time writer. It is, in any case, unusual for a publisher to renege on an agreement on grounds of unacceptability. A specialist non-fiction manuscript has to be pretty awful to be incapable of being knocked into shape by a combination of expert editing and rewriting. And remember, the *idea* of the book had to be good to get to this stage.

  Irrespective of what the agreement may say, however, there is no practical way by which a publisher can be *forced* to publish a book he no longer likes. If that happens, at least with an 'on delivery', rather than an 'on acceptance', clause you may get some financial compensation for your work.

- On publication. A cheque arriving with your six free copies may be pleasant, but personally I am happy at this stage to await the first sales-based royalty cheque.

Obviously, if the advance is paid at all three stages it is not going to be three times as much as a single advance; the advance amount is agreed and it is then either paid in full or in two or three parts. Advances should, of course, be non-returnable – except when the manuscript is never delivered.

The third important aspect of the agreement referred to above was an undertaking to publish. There are two parties to an agreement: each has his part to play. You contract to deliver a complete book manuscript, to the same quality as the sample, and on time. The publisher contracts to publish the book and to pay royalties. Understandably, this commitment is usually subject to wars, strikes and acts of God. It is customary for the clause about the publisher's commitment to publish to specify 'within a reasonable time' or 'with reasonable promptitude'. The best agreements – from the writer's viewpoint – put a time limit on the reasonable time. In my view this is gilt on the gingerbread: the publisher is unlikely to delay publication if he can avoid it – your book is an investment.

The best guarantee of the publisher's commitment to publish are his enthusiasm and the advance against future royalties that he pays you.

Other clauses

Other clauses in the agreement are of interest, although perhaps of less importance, at least to the first-time writer. Points to note include:

- You will be expected to indemnify the publisher against any infringement of copyright by you. This has already been mentioned in chapter 2.

- You will be expected to pay for the cost of excessive author's corrections – that is, if your corrections exceed 5, 10 or 15 per cent of the cost of the original typesetting. And even 15 per cent provides for a very small amount of corrections (see chapter 9).
- You will be given six free copies of your book, and the right to buy more copies – for your own use, not for sale – at, probably, $33\frac{1}{3}$ per cent discount. (The publisher may also let you buy copies of books by other writers in their list, at a similar discount. This is a very worth-while 'perk' – it is not usually mentioned in the agreement.) See chapter 9 for comments on the disposition of the six free copies.
- You will be required to agree not to write, contribute to, nor edit any other book for another publisher that would compete with your contracted book. This is an obvious business precaution and is clearly reasonable.
- You will often be expected to offer your next book to the same publisher. You may be glad of this entrée. You may, however, already be committed to another publisher for books of another type: the clause can and will be adjusted to allow for this. Or you can agree with the publisher to delete this clause altogether.
- There will be clauses about subsidiary rights. These are very important to some authors, but so far no one has yet made me an offer for the subsidiary rights in any of my non-fiction books. And no matter how I might dream of this book being made into a major TV documentary, I cannot see it ever happening!

Agents

With all these clauses in the agreement, which to some are worrying, and with your obvious wish to negotiate the best terms possible, should you employ an agent? There is little doubt that agents can press a publisher further towards the limit of what he will pay than an author would dare to do. The author always has that nagging worry that the publisher will just decide he is being too difficult and abandon the idea – the agent may negotiate more skilfully. The agent's idea of better terms will usually mean a bigger advance; the writer may be more interested in actually getting published than in early reward. I am sure that a writer is wrong to ignore or play down the importance of the reward, but I am not myself particularly concerned about the size of the advance, as long as I get one, as a 'commitment'.

Agents too will sometimes be able to 'feed' you with work. If they know your particular line of interest, they can put your name forward when they hear of a publisher launching a new series. One of my books started this way – the agent got me a big advance, but the book was soon 'remaindered'. And you will find – as I did – that colleagues delight in telling you they saw your book on a bargain counter.

Agents have their uses, but for the writer of one or two specialist non-fiction books they are, in my view, not so much a necessity as a nicety. More important, though, is whether or not an agent will want to work *with you.* It is most unlikely that an agent would take on a writer like you or I – there is not enough 'in it' for him. I no longer have an agent, although I did have one for a while. We parted by mutual consent, neither of us having made much money out of our association.

Agents make their money by taking a percentage – usually 10 per cent – of the writer's income. Let us suppose that the average royalty payment that I am going to get for a hardback book is 40 pence per book. The print run (number of copies printed in the first instance) may be, say, 5000 and take two years to sell. Five thousand copies at 40p each equals £2000 over two years. The agent's 10 per cent would amount to £30 from an advance of perhaps £300, and a further £170 over the next two years. Two hundred pounds does not buy many hours' work these days: and most certainly the £30 commission on the advance barely buys the time that would have to be spent negotiating the agreement.

If you are going to write a real block-buster – such as *How to win friends and influence people* or Samuelson's *Economics* – then an agent will be willing and very able to help you. If you are going to write *The Compleat Widget*, you may make money for yourself, but you do not need an agent, nor could you readily persuade one to represent you.

The publisher's sales questionnaire

You sold the idea for your book to the publisher; the publisher sells your book to the public. That is his job. He knows how best to do it and he is as interested in making money from your book as you are. But having said that, the professionally-minded writer helps the publisher all he can.

While you are writing the book, or perhaps before you start, the publisher will send you a sales questionnaire. This will include such questions and requests as:

- Describe in detail the reader(s) you had in mind while writing the book. Specify the reader's job and responsibilities, or his detailed interests. Specify also the magazines most appropriate to his job or hobby.
- Describe your book *in a single sentence*: say what it will do, and for whom.
- Describe your book in about two hundred words, as you would explain its relevance to a potential reader.
- Explain the ways in which your book meets a previously unmet need.
- List competing books and indicate how yours differs from them.
- Suggest academic courses – and institutions – that you would expect to use your book. Specify at which, if any, examination syllabuses your book is aimed.

- Suggest specialist journals that might be expected to review the book.
- Can you suggest any well-known people in your field, who might be willing to read your book in advance of publication, and endorse it for publicity purposes?
- Have you any other suggestions for promotion – seminars, local newspapers, personal contacts, etc.?
- Describe yourself, and your particular qualifications for writing the book, in about two hundred words.

Do NOT treat this market/sales questionnaire as just a nuisance. It is most important. Spend time and thought on completing it carefully and as fully as possible. It will help the publisher's sales force – who probably will not read the book itself – to talk knowledgeably about it and SELL it. You will, of course, have noticed how similar the questionnaire is to your own original 'sales package' and its associated preparation.

Do NOT assume that *everyone* knows that the leading academic body in your field is the RAW – the Regal Agglomeration of Widgeters. *You* know, it is your field; the publisher may not know. Tell him. Thence come sales, royalties, and kudos.

Book pricing

Sales are of course a function of the book's price. The publisher fixes the price of the book, using his commercial judgement to get it right. Too cheap means insufficient profit, too expensive means few sales. Much of the cost is a fixed input to his calculations.

The cost of this book for example, is made up of:

Editorial work	3%
Typesetting	6%
Printing, paper and binding	16%
Sales promotion	5%

Distribution and overheads	17%
Publisher's profit	10%
(from which tax and interest payments have to be met)	
Author's royalties	8%
Bookseller's discount	35%
UK retail price	100%

The bookseller's discount, the author's royalties, and the necessary profit margin are all more-or-less fixed. So too are distribution and overhead costs. Editorial costs can be kept down by persuading authors to produce their manuscripts in as near 'ready-to-typeset' form as possible – but there is not a great deal of scope here. As best he can, the publisher plays off typesetting costs against the other origination costs (origination comprises typesetting, printing, paper and binding costs) to fix the book price. Typesetting costs do not vary with the print-run: paper, printing and binding costs do. And it is basically the saving on further typesetting costs that enables the publisher to offer the 'royalty jump' – he has up to six per cent room for manoeuvre.

It is salutary to observe the relative proportions of the publisher's pre-tax (etc.) profit, the author's royalty and the bookseller's discount. The publisher is seldom grinding the poor author down as harshly as some writers think. Their shares are not dissimilar – for which one provides the content of the book and the other bears the risk and the cost of producing it. (But this commercial awareness in no way inhibits my attempts to squeeze better terms out of the publisher whenever I can. After all, the publisher's 10 per cent on the retail price is, more realistically, just over 20 per cent on his capital outlay.)

Many writers, over-anxious to keep the price of their book down, wonder why the publisher does not bring it out as a paperback. The economics of paperback production are directly related to the size of the print-run. Non-fiction books of a technical or semi-technical nature seldom warrant more than five thousand copies at the initial print – and my fairly specialist engineering books have had even smaller initial print-runs. At this scale, the production and binding processes for a paperback are nearly the same as for a hard-back – the only saving is in the small extra cost of the hard cover. But book-buyers *expect* paperbacks to be significantly cheaper.

It is only when a big print-run can be achieved that the cost of the book can be brought right down by adopting a paperback format. Few 'real' paperbacks are produced in smaller print-runs than 20 000 copies – and paperback publishers make their big profits from books with print-runs in the hundreds of thousands.

Look at the spine of this relatively expensive paperback, of a 'real' – that is, cheap – paperback, and of a hard-back book. This book and the hard-back have their pages bound in groups or sections of folded and sewn sheets; the cheap paperback does not. Paperbacks are what is known as 'perfect' bound: each page is separately held in the book, and to the paper binding, by glue or plastic. This book and the hard-back are made up of 'signatures', which is the technical term for the sections of (usually) sixteen pages, folded from a single printed sheet.

When a publisher is first considering the printing of a book, he will investigate setting it out so that it fits into a multiple of sixteen pages. Take any hard-back book from your shelves and add the number of preliminary pages to the numbered pages. The result will usually be a multiple of sixteen.

The sales campaign

How does the publisher sell your book? Part of his effort may go into persuading booksellers to stock it and academics to recommend it, but this is 'hidden' activity. What the writer sees of the sales campaign are the advertisements, the reviews and the mailing brochure.

Many first-time writers expect their books to be widely advertised; they are surprised by the almost total lack of advertising of this type. Publishers view advertisements of fairly narrow-interest non-fiction books more as a means of promoting the publishing house name than as a specific sales 'pitch'. Advertisements of 'our' type of non-fiction book are seldom cost-effective.

Reviews of your book will help sales. This is one of the reasons why your careful completion of the publisher's marketing questionnaire is so important. But you will not get as many reviews as you think. The quality Sunday papers will not review your book, nor will the national daily papers. Even your local paper may ignore your literary masterpiece unless they need something to fill in a vacant space in the paper. You can hope, with some confidence, for a review in the specialist journal(s) devoted to the subject of your book. Even this will not appear for several months – so do not hold your breath while waiting for it. Many reviews will be little more than four or five lines; others will be mere repetition of the 'blurb'. Some, one hopes few, reviews will be bad: develop a thick skin, even a bad review can improve sales as long as it is not too bad. (There is an apposite old show-biz saying that it does not matter what they say as long as they get your name right.)

For some books – depending partly on the sales attitude and ethics of the publisher – a mailed brochure incorporating an order form is a major part of the sales campaign. Some publishers avoid mail campaigns because of the inevitable conflict of interests with the booksellers' trade, but the publisher can do a lot of direct sales promotion within the cost limits of the booksellers' discount. As the writer, you will have no control over this, but it is useful to appreciate the use and problems of mailed brochure campaigns. (Most brochures repeat the book's front cover in their layout.)

However the sales are obtained, their pattern over time will be fairly consistent: at publication there will be a large number of sales, but this will soon fall off sharply. The ideal book is one that then settles down to a steady – and not too small – sales level thereafter. Figure 10.1 graphs typical sales figures, based on one of my books.

The publication of your book can sometimes lead you on to other associated activities. I have recently been asked to talk to one-day seminars about effective management communications and technical writing. As well as being paid for this work, there were associated sales for my book *How to Communicate*. Such seminars entail a lot of preparatory

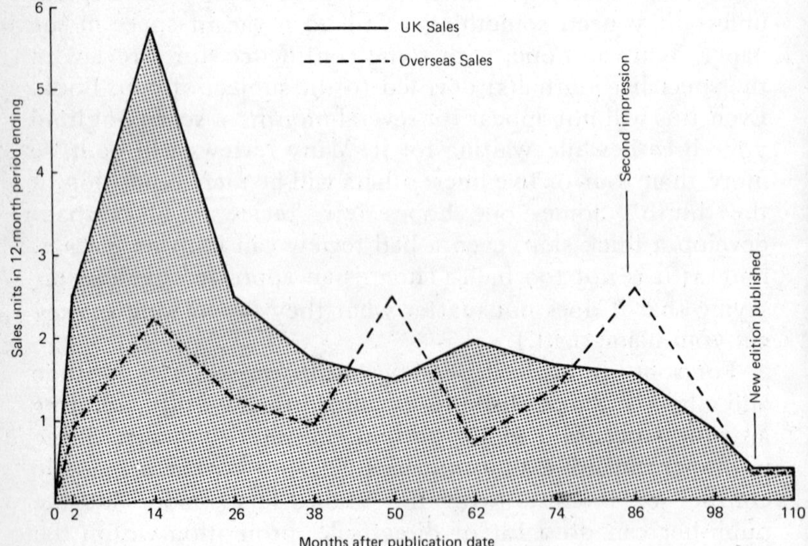

Fig 10.1 The pattern of sales for one of my books, typical of many such technical non-fiction books. The most important characteristic is the levelling-off of the home sales, sometimes enhanced by the less consistent overseas sales.

work however, and may give you stage-fright – they MUST be slick and professional. There is also the possibility of evening class courses based on your book; they pay less well but nevertheless they do aid sales. Some particularly popular non-fiction books can lead to (paid) radio and/or television appearances – but I have never achieved such fame or fortune. I suspect such opportunities are rare for the specialist or technical non-fiction writer.

If you hear of seminars or courses being organised in 'your' subject, for which you think your book would be particularly appropriate – with or without your personal involvement – you should notify your publisher. The sales manager can make contact with the organisers of any such activity that you identify; some of these contacts can lead to orders. But be wary of inundating the sales manager with only remote possibilities.

Managing your writing income

Even if you only write one book and have no other associated spare time income – such as from talks about your book – it is well worth your while to keep comprehensive accounts. If you are unsuccessful it will tell you how much your hobby is costing you – and perhaps persuade you to collect butterflies instead. If you are successful you will need to deal with the tax authorities.

Keep accounts of expenditure incurred on research and other preparation for your book before you even start writing it or seeking a publisher. The tax man may not at that time accept you as a writer, nor the expenses as a charge against income, but once you start earning royalties you may be able to claim back-expenses. You should certainly set all current expenses against writing income, declaring both in full.

I record my writing income and expenditure in what is known as a Petty Cash accounts book. The way in which I use this book gives me one cash column for the few, irregular, cash receipts, and a lot of cash columns for the continual expenditure. I use one expenditure column for totalling, recording here every penny spent on anything connected with writing. I then *repeat* these entries on one or more other columns which break down the expense into several broad headings – enabling me to categorise the expenditure annually for my tax claim. My analysis columns are headed:

- postage (the most used)
- research (photocopies, etc.)
- stationery
- travel
- others (expenses not significant or frequent enough to warrant listing separately)

Because I am interested in how I spend my 'writing' money, I *again* repeat a categorisation of all expenditure in further columns, headed with the names of the projects on which I am currently working. But perhaps this is over-enthusiasm.

If and when your writing activities extend beyond the first book it may be worth seeking the services of an accountant to advise on tax aspects. If you do not explore all legitimate ways of reducing the tax on your writing you are foolish, not professional. Tax evasion is illegal; tax avoidance is not. As an indication of the expenses that might be allowable, the Tax Inspector has accepted my claims for:

- telephone rental, for receiving calls
- car mileage: I claim at rates per mile that are standard in the public sector
- my wife's assistance, taking messages, filing papers and checking drafts
- the replacement of my typewriter and my pocket calculator
- the expansion of my filing system.

Future work

You have written your book, it is published, and it rests on many bookshelves. What now? You are involved, you cannot just pack your bags and steal away. You MUST keep up-to-date in your subject in case the publisher requires a second edition of your book. And let us immediately clarify the difference between *impressions* and *editions.* When a book is first published the initial print run is an *impression.* When that is sold out the publisher can make further printings or impressions of the original material – with effectively no change in the text, although if there are minor errors they can be corrected before a second impression is printed. A new *edition* entails up-dating, revision and often considerable re-setting.

If and when you come to preparing a second edition of your book, approach this as a new exercise. Do not merely add new material: old material will require deletion and the conclusions or the logic may also need rethinking. Review the whole logic of the book's structure: can this too now be improved in the light of later knowledge? At the same time, remember that it is a new edition you are preparing – not a totally new book. You should retain the same target readers and methods of reaching them. If you feel the need to write a different book for a different audience – do so by all means, but not within the old original.

Without waiting for the publisher to call for a new edition, you may find that you have caught the writing bug. Having finished your first book you want to keep writing and to write another book. As long as you have the *content* in you – that is, as long as you can write about what you *know*, rather than turn into a mere hack – turn back to page one in this book and off you go. And your experiences with your first book may have suggested ways of improving on my recommended methods, ways in which you, personally, can work better. You will then be writing your book your way – which is good. I will stick to my methods – they suit me.

There is room for us both.

Summary

(1) Agreements between publisher and author are fairly standard. The most important clauses from the viewpoint of the new author are those specifying length and delivery date, royalty rates and advance payments, and committing the publisher to publish the book.

(2) A royalty rate of 10 per cent of the published UK price on UK sales is fairly common. Overseas sales and paperback publications usually attract a lower rate of royalty payment. When sales increase sufficiently, it is not unusual for the royalty rate to be raised, usually by 2½ per cent.

(3) Authors should seek a non-returnable advance payment against future royalties. The size of this advance is variable but its payment is an implied commitment by the publisher. The advance is often paid part on signing the agreement and part on delivery of the manuscript.

(4) Agents are not necessary for the new writer of a fairly specialist non-fiction book – and they would seldom be interested in taking on such a writer anyway. They usually take 10 per cent of the writer's earnings for their services.

(5) The publisher's sales questionnaire is of great importance: you, the writer, should know where the best, or extra markets for your book are to be found. You should work with the publisher: the more sales he makes, the greater your royalty payments and your kudos.

(6) Do not expect your book to be the subject of a major advertising campaign – it will not be. Nor will it get as many reviews as you expect – and they won't all be

good ones. Some publishers rely considerably on mailed brochures incorporating order forms.

(7) You should welcome any extra activities associated with your book – seminars and courses mean sales, even though they also mean more work for you.

(8) Every writer should record all his writing and associated research expenditure, as well as his writing income. The tax-man will want details of expenses before allowing tax reliefs.

(9) Keep up-to-date with your subject in readiness for a second edition.

(10) If you have caught the writing bug and now want to write more, for the pleasure of it – welcome, and good luck!

Appendix 1

The writer's library

Every writer will build up a comprehensive library of books on his specialist subject(s). The content of this library is, of course, unique to each writer. But all non-fiction writers can benefit from the possession of a few books associated with the writing process itself. The following list is by no means complete or exclusive – it is no more than a list of the books that I find useful myself.

- *Writers' & Artists' Yearbook* (London: A & C Black, annually). An indispensable handbook for any non-fiction writer. Apart from listing almost every book-publisher in the United Kingdom and a goodly selection in America, Australia, Canada, Ireland, India, South Africa and New Zealand, it contains advice on a multitude of other subjects. There are short features on copyright, libel and income tax. There are lists of societies and clubs of particular interest to writers and there are longer features on the more important of these. There are even a few pages on how to prepare and submit a book to a publisher. Very good value for money – an annual necessity.
- A conventional dictionary – my own is *The Concise Oxford Dictionary* (Oxford University Press, 6/e 1978.) An excellent dictionary in almost continual use. I check meanings

and spellings and frequently find that my preconceptions are misconceptions. Always get the new edition of the dictionary as soon as it is published – the English language is constantly changing.

- *Roget's Thesaurus* – my version is the Penguin Reference Book edition. This is the complement of the dictionary. A dictionary explains the meaning of a known word. Roget enables you to start from an idea and, with patience, decide on just the right word. But beware that you do not become a slave to the Thesaurus, forever dredging in new words. Always remember that the simple words, qualified as and if necessary, are the best. Your object is to communicate information – not to impress.
- *The Oxford Dictionary for Writers and Editors* (Oxford University Press, 5/e 1986). An invaluable source for authoritative advice on preferred and/or 'tricky' spelling, preferred abbreviations, meanings of abbreviations, first names and dates of birth and death of famous people, and even advice on how to punctuate. Once you have a copy you will wonder how you managed so long without it.
- Hart, Horace, *Hart's Rules for Compositors and Readers* (Oxford University Press, 38/e 1978). The companion to the Authors' & Printers' Dictionary, Hart's Rules is a very readable book rather than a dictionary. Advice in it includes, for example, when and where to use capitals, where to divide a word, how to set out an index, and much well-illustrated advice on how to use various punctuation marks. A good read – no matter how much you know already.
- *Dictionary of Quotations* – my copy is by D. G. Browning, in the Everyman's Library, published by J. M. Dent, London, 1951. There are others of equal merit, such as that published by Penguin. Every now and then you will wish to include a time-honoured phrase in your writing – reference to a dictionary of quotations will ensure that you get it right.

And three guides to good writing style:

- Fowler H. W. (revised by Gowers, Sir Ernest) *A Dictionary of Modern English Usage* (Oxford University Press 2/e 1968)
- Gowers, Sir Ernest *The Complete Plain Words* (Her Majesty's Stationery Office, London, 2/e 1973.)
- Gunning, Robert *The Technique of Clear Writing* (McGraw-Hill, New York, Rev/e 1968)

Three magnificent books that, in completely different ways, put across the same essential characteristics of good writing – simplicity, clarity and precision.

And since this book was written, there is now, from the same pen, the invaluable:

- Wells, Gordon *The Book Writer's Handbook* (Allison & Busby/W. H. Allen 1989). This book, which is to be updated from time to time, is a market guide for authors. It contains page-long reports on around a hundred of the best, largely non-specialist, British publishers who consider (and sometimes accept) unsolicited books from new writers. It summarises their editorial policies, the categories they publish – and how much you might get paid. And it demonstrates, once again, the opportunities there are, particularly for non-fiction writers.

Appendix 2

Symbols for correcting proofs

Make corrections in ink, in the margins – marks in the text should indicate where the correction is to be made.

To make a correction, cross out the existing letter(s) in the text and write in the margin the letter(s) to be substituted, followed by a stroke (/).

If a number of corrections are to be made in one line, divide them between left and right-hand margins (their order reading from left to right in each margin); individual corrections should be separated by a stroke (/).

Any other comments or instructions you write on the proofs should be circled, with the word PRINTER clearly written in capitals.

MARK IN MARGIN	MEANING	CORRESPONDING MARK IN THE TEXT
extra matter followed by /	insert the extra matter in text	⋏
₰	delete	cross out the part to be deleted
₰	delete and close up	cross out the part to be deleted, and use ⊂⊃
stet	reinstate as printed	. . . . . . dots under part of text to be reinstated
ital	change to italics	underline characters to be altered

MARK IN MARGIN	MEANING	CORRESPONDING MARK IN THE TEXT
s.c.	change to small capitals	double-underline characters to be altered
caps	change to capital letters	treble-underline characters to be altered
c.&.s.c.	capitals (for initial letters) and small capitals	≡ under initials, = under the rest
bold	use bold type	∿∿ under the part to be altered
l.c.	change to lower case type	encircle affected parts
rom.	change to roman type	encircle affected parts
w.f.	wrong fount – use the correct fount	encircle affected parts
◎	invert	encircle affected parts
×	replace damaged characters	encircle affected parts
⌄	replace with 'superior' characters	/ for substitution, ⋏ for insertion
⌃	replace with 'inferior' characters	/ for substitution, ⋏ for insertion
underline	insert underline	underline affected parts
⁀	close up by deleting space between characters	⁀
#	insert space between characters	⋏
#	insert space between lines	>

MARK IN MARGIN	MEANING	CORRESPONDING MARK IN THE TEXT
less #	reduce space between characters	/
less #	reduce space between lines	(
equal #	make space appear equal	/
trs.	transpose	⌐ between parts to be transposed; use numbers if there is any chance of confusion
centre	move to centre	indicate the correct position with ⌐ ¬
□	indent one em space	⊏
□□	indent two em spaces	⊏
⊏	move over to right	⊏
⊐	move over to left	⊐
move	move material to new position	[ ] to show where
take over	take over material to next line, column or page	⊏
take back	take back material to previous line, column or page	⊐
raise	move lines up	↑ to show where
lower	move lines down	↓ to show where
‖	align vertically	‖

MARK IN MARGIN	MEANING	CORRESPONDING MARK IN THE TEXT
═══	straighten lines	through the affected lines
⊥	push down space	encircle affected space
n.p.	start new paragraph	[
run on	remove new paragraph to allow text to run on	⊃
spell out	spell out in full	encircle affected parts
out: see copy	insert the omitted parts of the copy (which should be returned with the proof)	⋏
,/	insert comma	/ for substitution ⋏ for insertion
⊙	insert full stop	/ for substitution ⋏ for insertion
:/ ;/ (as required)	insert semicolon (or colon)	/ for substitution ⋏ for insertion

Appendix 3
Word Processing for Authors

Word processors have suddenly – largely thanks to Alan Sugar, the boss of Amstrad – come within the financial reach of ordinary writers.

Many authors have already invested in 'an Amstrad' – the package sold as the Amstrad PCW8256, 8512 or 9512. Despite fears of not being able to understand the technology, just about everyone manages to get their Amstrad working; and, within days, cannot imagine life without it.

But a word processor need not be 'an Amstrad'. You can put together your own set of equipment. Indeed, if you want anything faster, more flexible, than the PCW range, it is necessary to assemble the equipment piece by piece.

To put together your own equipment – and to better understand the operation of the packaged PCWs – it helps to know a little about the components. And it helps to understand the jargon, which can otherwise overwhelm.

Strictly speaking, a word processor is the computer program that makes the equipment work. But in everyday terms, a word processor consists of:

- a keyboard – like a conventional typewriter but with extra keys;
- a monitor – a screen which displays your words as you key them in;
- a computer – the electronic box of tricks that makes it all work;
- a storage device – customarily one or more disk-drives;
- a printer – which accepts electronic instructions and transfers them to paper, as conventional typescript; and
- the word processor – a computer program which causes the equipment to work in a word processing mode.

The Keyboard

As well as the QWERTY keys, a computer keyboard has a set of 'function' keys and an *Enter* key. There are other 'new' keys, but they are of less importance.

The ten or more function keys (labelled F1, F2, etc) are used to operate the program. As an example, with my program and equipment, F1 brings up a screenful of helpful advice; F3 followed by an appropriate letter lets me print, erase, change margins or line spacing, etc; F4 changes the typeface; and so on.

The *Enter* key, easily mistaken initially for a 'carriage return' key, serves two main purposes. It marks the end of a paragraph and/or tells the computer to implement an instruction. It is not used at the end of a line; as you type, the program automatically moves onto the next line as each successive line fills up. This is called 'word wrap'. It is exactly like typing on a single, paragraph-long, line and is one of the ways in which word processing is faster than conventional typing.

The Monitor

As you type on the keyboard, your words appear on a screen in front of you. There is a tiny oblong, or a flashing underline mark, the *cursor*, which indicates where the next character will appear. If you need to correct something, you move the *cursor* to where you want to type – using four arrowed keys – and again, just type. You can either insert letters or overwrite them.

Monitor screens for word processors can be monochrome – black-and-white or green or amber – or coloured. Colour, as always costs more than monochrome and is sometimes thought to be distracting for word processing. It certainly isn't essential.

The Computer

A computer consists of a multitude of tiny switches – which can be on or off. The switches are grouped in batches of eight. Eight on/off options allow 128 different settings – in one system, a capital G is represented by off–on–off–off–off–on–on–on. (This is usually represented as the binary number 01000111.) A set of eight switches is known as a *byte*. The capacity of a computer is measured in thousands of bytes: *kilobytes* or just K. A computer with 8000 switches therefore has a memory of 1K (very small).

The Amstrad PCW8256 has a memory – Random Access Memory (RAM for short) – of 256K, or 256,000 bytes. Similarly, the Amstrad PCW9512 has a RAM of 512K – that's how Mr Sugar code-names his machines.

A computer's memory works fine all the time the power is switched on. You load the word processor program into RAM and the remainder, maybe half, of the memory space is then available for your written work. When you want to switch off the power though, you either 'save' your work – or you lose it.

The Storage

Just as music can be recorded onto a cassette, computer data – our written words – can be stored electronically. It is stored on disks which are 'played' in disk drives: you insert the disk, in its protective sleeve, turn a switch to hold it in, and it is ready to 'play'.

The word processor program (*see* below) comes on a disk; the computer has to read in these instructions before it can be used. (You tell the computer to 'load' it.) When you want to stop writing, you 'save' the words, from the computer's memory (the RAM), onto a disk – just like recording onto a cassette. Next day, you again 'load' the wp program *and* the half-finished work – and carry on from where you left off.

When your work is finished, you will want to print it. (Computer people talk of making a 'hard copy'.) A few key-strokes and your work is sent to your printer – and printed. And you still have an electronic copy, on disk.

The Printer

There are various types of printer which will work with a word processor. Ink-jet and laser printers produce very high quality typescript – but are expensive. Most writers will choose between a daisy-wheel or dot-matrix printer.

A daisy-wheel printer operates on the same principle as a typewriter: type keys strike an inked ribbon which marks the paper. The difference is that the type characters are set on the ends of tiny arms projecting from a central hub – it looks (*very* vaguely) like petals on a daisy. Hence daisy-wheel. The computer 'instructs' the printer to spin the wheel to bring the required character under a tiny hammer, which then hits it onto the ribbon. The result is conventional typescripts.

A dot-matrix printer can operate much faster than a daisy-wheel. It works in a different fashion. A dot-matrix printer has a 'print head' from which an upright line of tiny wires projects onto the ribbon, and then onto the paper. The computer 'tells' the printing head which wires to push out. Each projecting wire produces a dot on the paper; the ink-dots form the required character.

Early dot-matrix printers used a 9-pin print head operating in a 9 × 7 matrix. The print head moves along the paper a fraction at a time, printing whichever of the 9 dots are required by each character. The result is 'dotty'. Until recently, many publishers refused to accept manuscripts produced on a dot-matrix printer. To improve the quality of dot-matrix printing, machines were designed that would – effectively – double-strike; the print head moves fractionally up after each 9-pin strike, and strikes again, to fill in the gaps between the dots. This is known as 'near letter quality' (NLQ) printing – and is more-or-less acceptable.

The latest development in dot-matrix printing is the 24-pin print head. This works just like the 9-pin machine – but with 24 dots, the result is almost indistinguishable from conventional typescript. A 24-pin printer is highly recommended to any author.

The Word Processor

Although it is customary to refer to the whole set of equipment as 'the word processor', this title should more correctly be reserved for the program. The word processor program comes on a disk and 'instructs' the computer how to operate. The program allows you to move words around on the screen, to 'store' them, and to send them to the printer.

There are many word processor programs. One, Locoscript, is supplied with the Amstrad PCW8256 package. Different programs offer different advantages: a businessman's program is not necessarily the best for an author, and an article-writer might find another even better; you must shop around.

Any good program should offer most of the following:

- A 'what you see is what you get' (WYSIWYG) display on the screen.
- The ability to write a 'file' (a chapter perhaps) of at least 5000 words (say 45K) within RAM and to move the cursor about quickly within this.
- The ability to insert, remove or transfer anything from a single character to a whole page anywhere within the document.
- A 'search and replace' facility – automatically changing a word or phrase, throughout a document. (Used by novelists to change a character's name.)
- The ability to print single pages from within a multi-page document.
- An ongoing, and preferably always on-screen, word count.
- A spelling checker, offering suggested corrections.

Many word processors offer more than the above; few offer less. You must look at what a program offers and how it will suit your own way of working. I use the QUILL program (from Psion's PC-4 suite), which has no spelling check – but has other facilities that suit my working methods.

Word processors are the quill pens of today. Every writer should learn to use one – it's not difficult. Once used, you will never go back.

Index